THE CREST RIDERS
-EXPECTATIONS-

A

Novel

By

Street Endie

Illustrations and cover art by Street Endie

Street Endie © 2013, Poet's Arcade Inc.

ISBN: 978-0-615-89666-3

To my family

To my teachers and to my friends

THE SIBLINGS SAGA

Track listings.

1 – The Legend of Tessa Seredin

Zionée touched the spot on the mantle of her Japanese sailor outfit where the Hiragana characters of her name spiked into shape like beats in a lifeline. As she stood on the shores, she stared into the rippling glass. Possessing a tightly clenched face that would otherwise be beautiful if it could know how to smile, Zionée's green eyes sparkled in the mirror of foam and salt. Her shoes rested on the sand with her socks tucked inside of them. Standing a couple feet away, her little brother Edin pointed to the golden horizon where a small burst of splashes was making its way towards them. Zionée clenched her fists. The ocean tugged the water against her cold, wet ankles, withdrawing another salty ghost before her eyes. Her breathing quickened as she fought down a rising urge to drown someone.

They had only a matter of hours against the many miles they had left to get back to school in time. Sheltevue High was located at the bottom of a suburban chasm surrounded by a villa of convenient store markets and vintage entertainment centers. The main building was a century-old, gothic cake of multiple stories. In the middle of it was a bell tower, which loomed mute above its checkered kingdom. Much of the school's internal departments were layered across a large slope including the auditorium and the science building, which connected to the library, cafeteria, and art building.

A year ago, the new principal sat alone at a circular table far across the edge of the teacher's lounge. Hidden behind towers of district reports and former homework assignments, Tiffanie Flores sipped her drink quietly while playing games on her calculator. She wore a snappy purple suit, had dark, curled hair, and a richly tanned complexion. As her high score continued to climb, her attention drifted to the conversation of the teachers sitting a table away.

"Can you believe her?" one of them said. "Where did she find the audacity to make us take the AP exams?"

After tearing open an AP exam packet with her teeth, Flores took out her number two pencil and quietly began taking the subject test and timing herself as though she were a student. She was careful to spend about a minute on each problem and to skip the ones she could not risk guessing. When she finished, she walked up to the invisible proctor in the empty school gym and placed the test sheet down. Then she put on her hoodie and attempted to do a layup from the middle of the court when suddenly the door opened so she promptly dribbled the other way, pretending to be returning a stray ball. One by one, all her staff took the AP exams corresponding to the courses they taught. When they finished, they exited the indoor gym and awkwardly avoided her gaze. A week later, she published their results online for them to see but made it optional for them to show their students. She half suspected that this was one of the reasons she would not be joining the laughter of her colleagues sitting a table away that day.

Flores put down her calculator and started putting away her things in her book bag. Since the former Principal Debra Abrams left her post from graduating onto superintendant, she had issued a series of controversial new programs to cultivate a more unified school spirit. As the youngest principal the school had ever seen, she was prompt and ambitious, barely running out of her thirties from a decade-long distraction of medical school. It had taken a while for her to assert her leadership over her diverse and quirky staff. Although the history teacher usually said good morning to her, none of the others spoke to her outside of meetings. For several professional development days, Flores worked hard to be a force worth reckoning with until came the disastrous loss of friction between her tennis shoes and some spilled mash potato. She had fallen over backwards and dropped all her food from her cafeteria tray. Her pants were stained with her spilled soda and her suit was smudged with some taco sauce. Their laughter was brief and casual but for some reason it still sounded loud and hurtful. Flores clenched the dropped cafeteria napkin with her sticky palm, feeling more like a fool than a principal.

Some of the teachers got up and left their table without saying goodbye to each other. The superintendant accused her of fueling unwanted tension between them with her AP stunt by forbidding Flores access to the newest school fund reports. But the crafty principal, who had once caught a student hacking the Sheltevue district server, broke in by herself online. As she went over the lists of funds, Flores noticed that the academic resources were pooled favorably towards one half of the school. The other half of it that tested into the normal curriculum was increasingly cast in an inferior light. To combat this, she created several programs to prepare it for reunification. But with the student media barely being persuaded to represent the whole school and with the sports teams segregated between sectors, progress was not coming easy.

As a magnet school, Sheltevue divided its curriculum between two groups: publics and privates. The hallways of the private sector were usually without the stains of gum or weathered graffiti that contaminated the rest of the school. Under the discreet instruction of the superintendant, the janitors made sure that these sectors looked as immaculate as the records of the students with classes in them. The corridors were full of shiny, white lockers outlined in blue. Alternating between these floors was the urban cavity surviving on the ghosts of yesteryear budgets. Full of dented lockers and sprawling graffiti, the public sectors were legible with the effects of its overpopulated traffic. It was easy to read where the violence was absorbed, where shoulders were crushed, and where the angry ink dried with time. A line of glass above the lockers streamed across the halls, connecting the two sectors with a gradient of dust to color.

Flores often ate alone in her office. The paper work mounted relentlessly on her desk. During lunch and nutrition, she started habitually peering out of her window after sighing with exasperation. A bee hit the glass with a small thud and she saw it do a somersault down before restarting its wings like an engine and zipping off again. Although there was no dress code, the privates were becoming easier to tell apart from the publics. They seemed more animate and dispersed in little groups rather than clumped together in forced squads of protective bullying. They also appeared more politically relaxed with their diversity than others could afford to be. The privates lived off of the expectations of their parents, universal unto themselves, that they were smarter, more athletic, and better. But what was most striking to the principal was the expectation that they were, and so often appeared to be, happier. She turned back to her desk and widened her eyes, moving a pile of district reports aside and opening her program journal, feverishly writing up something that could finally challenge their humility. The leftover takeout on her desk continued to spice the air. Flores slammed her fist to her table excitedly after she finished writing.

It was their attitude.

During the last days of her freshman year, Zionée Dunnelin walked through the hallway and heard her classmates talking about something new. Her pace was always deliberate with not a muscle wasted on feeling insecure, constantly moving between her classes, her athletics, and her clubs. She noticed a brunette with a butterfly hairpin talking to a dark-haired, freckly girl as she was closing her locker.

"We sign up and average our grades together for a combined score with two other people."

"Who'd want to risk something like that?"

The brunette clicked her hairpin so that the wings could flap twice as she replaced it somewhere else on her head. "It could be a fun thing to do with friends."

"Fun way to lose them, you mean," the dark-haired girl scoffed. "What if you suck?"

"Yeah, but we're in the magnet. Compared to some people, maybe we could use a little teamwork."

"Oh yeah?"

Her dark-haired friend noticed the subject of their conversation enlarge in the glass mirror on her locker.

"Because that girl, Zionée? You hear about her? They say

anyone within a fifteen-feet radius of her can instantly feel their dreams of becoming valedictorian be crushed," the brunette girl said, before noticing her friend stare past her. "What?"

"You might want to stand fifteen feet away," said Zionée.

The girl scoffed at her before opening her locker over her face. A different person, place, and time ago, the butterfly-pin brunette had invited her in on a friendly joke during class. But whoever she and her new friend is now, Zionée could not bother to keep up.

She continued her way to the principal's office located down the hall next to the trophy cabinet. When she stepped into the minty, new room she noticed that the posters of Cesar Chavez and the Spice Girls were now on the ground.

"You taking those down?"

"The superintendant said it was inappropriate."

Zionée popped her eyebrows at her in a sarcastic manner.

"So," Flores smiled and nodded at her. "You get the email?"

"Yeah."

Zionée labored on the thought of telling her that she didn't have any friends.

"So should I do it?"

Flores shrugged and stared at her. For an awkwardly still minute, they both didn't say a word. Zionée finally sighed, relenting.

"Come on," the principal smiled.

"Friends are where most people would go looking."

"But you're not most people."

Flores frowned and nodded, consenting to the exception she was insisting for her to make in her eyes.

Zionée walked out on campus and glared at everybody she passed by, maintaining her opinion of them being stupid and unworthy. She got out of the hallway after passing by the glitter of trophies, half the luster owed to her from last year's achievements. Sitting at one of the square benches that surrounded the tall trees in the courtyard was Edin.

As much as the small growth spurt, black hair, boyish face, and gray-blue eyes risked the secrecy of his age, Edin was as academically impeccable as his sister was. Under her careful tutelage, he had skipped several grades so that he could start high school in time for her sophomore year. Zionée walked up to him and he opened his backpack to show her his half-eaten lunch.

"You got a minute?"

Edin finished the application with a blue pen and then took out his phone and texted his sister. Sitting by the cold, black kitchen panels, Zionée sipped her bubble tea and took out her phone. After a moment, she put down the phone and made a one-note tisking sound out of her mouth. Earlier that day, a girl with sunny blonde hair on her soccer team approached her at the bench. Zionée was halfway through spiking her drink with performance-enhancing substances when she appeared next to her.

"Hey, captain," she asked. "Is that my drink?"

Zionée quickly took a sip of it but did not gulp. She shook her head and squinted at her.

"You know how we're supposed to take turns introducing our new teammates to our parents at conferences?"

Zionée nodded.

"Why do you never have the same set of parents?"

Several heads spun in their direction. There was a malicious smile on her lead striker Debby. After the goalie left her sight, Zionée spat the spiked water out.

In the kitchen, she finished rinsing her mouth by the sink after eating. Then she walked back to her phone where the page rested on the article she was denying her mind's appetite as though the very letters were a carefully crafted poison.

Tessa Seredin.

Her image spat back Zionée's own on the center of the page. Immediately, she and her brother were both walking out of the door and on their way to the library. The aqueous stain of night was already spreading across the pale sky. Edin took the second glance at the photo that his sister did not.

When they got there, Zionée left him waiting at the main lobby. Reading the weight of her footsteps made, he chose to stay by a table near the entrance to wait. Although their features were eerily similar, the photo was in black and white. Zionée's eyes were a deep olive; determined and always fitted to a subtle but guarded scowl. Although she chose not to read the article, in the first weeks of school, bits and pieces launched by her classmates and teachers mercilessly organized the contents together in her head against her will.

"She was a revolutionary…"

"…Just some glorified overachiever."

"…She was like this legend. Impossible to live up to."

"According to the date, she's probably as old as our parents."

"Have you seen the girl who looks like her?"

Zionée lifted her head from her arms at that last comment but they had all turned away quickly enough to avoid her scowl. The teacher was allowing fifteen minutes of free discussion on the English essay they were doing.

"They say she had a brother. A twin."

"Really?"

"Their names were identical. Tesla."

"Sounds like a coincidence."

"A coincidence Tessa supposedly wasn't stupid about."

"Yeah, if I had a twin…"

Zionée was uncertain of when she stopped listening and when she began dreaming. In a subconscious trespass, these new ingredients brewed excitedly with the growing mental picture of her possible mother.

"That's the new kid hanging around your turf, Yo."

Alonzo Rico nudges at his friend Derrion Yogun. Yogun, a senior, is African-American of the first generation and speaks with a slight lingering Zimbabwe accent. His friend Alonzo is Latin American with a little facial hair and wears old leather-clad attire.

The classroom is riddled with the verbal pollution of vile insults from kids with insecurities of all shapes and sizes. Sitting at the corner is the newest one, with an effeminate face masking a quiet anger trembling in the still. He is armored in dirty, blue denim and gloved hands with fierce eyes staring from under an old, immigrant cap. The teacher walks out into the hallway to chat with the security officers. Sometimes Yogun steps in and calms everything out but today is one of those days he sits back quietly and reads. With only a few community college classes short of graduation, he is smart to how little else there is to gain from getting involved with enrollment-risking conflicts. But as the gang leader of one of the toughest crowds in Sheltevue, he does not need to be as directly involved. At the start of every semester is a crop of new faces. They arrive shaking in their seats becoming the test subjects to horrific insults and provocation. Whatever their social or cultural facets, injustice does not discriminate. Yogun runs his fingers through his dreadlocks; casually bored by all the ignorant evil his classmates awkwardly flex their social skills with. Their rundown classroom is almost always home to this anarchy.

"Some girly-sounding name no one cares to remember," Alonzo finally answers after he asks a couple kids seated nearby.

"Nobody heard it in role call?"

Alonzo shakes his head.

"Just some new meat. Leave the white boy alone. He'll settle in on his own."

"Uh, he's settlin'," Alonzo says, pointing.

The quick eruption of noise and the teacher shouting "stop" makes Yogun stir and to his bewilderment, this "Tessa", a feminine version of the boy's name that the other kids are shouting as an insult to his masculinity, is already caught in a brawl.

Her fists fly violently and illiterately in several directions. Bruises and blood loss send signals sharpening to the bone. The agony is illuminating. She takes some of the hits that her expensive martial arts training could have easily saved her from. Her classmates roar with bloodthirsty enthusiasm as one of the ceiling lights flicker. The violence and pain collects against her senses faster than they can register. Like a stampede, the hate and anger starts to fester inside. After a crushing smack to the face she falls over and picks herself back up to return an uppercut to the nearest attacker. Then, riding on the energy of the same pain in her jaw, she turns around and coldly decks him off his feet. As he falls to the ground bleeding, Tessa snorts a little blood of her own to remember not to feel sorry. Another thug tries to grab her from behind but she meticulously catches his thumbs and twists them. He doubles back in pain and she turns around and swings her elbow at his face. Then she is hit in the back of her head by the other one and falls over. Quickly, she kicks up and breaks one of their hands with her foot. Then she rolls back on her feet, swinging her fist hard into the other one's diaphragm. She blocks his returning blow at the expense of her wrist bone and then throws another punch straight up to his face. As he falls, she stands up and walks over to him and starts kicking down at him until the police pull her away.

The class bell rings.

Tessa is escorted with hard, cold metal biting around her wrists. The light rain stings and cleans her bloodied face. She walks forward, staring determinedly at nobody while dripping with a rising price tag of a medical bill. They guide her through the messy cafeteria courtyard. All eyes of the public world are now on her. She whistles the last few ounces of blood out the side of her mouth.

Zionée arrived to English class the next day and sat down by the corner right seat near the front of the classroom. In the window next to her she caught the reflection of her classmate who was sitting a few seats away, Rigley Kurosawa. He had messy, black hair and his eyes were timber, filtered see-through by the dark, tinted window. Rigley, who although was half-Chinese and half-Japanese, spoke with an incessant English accent, which nobody knew for certain how he got. He often performed meekly under the standards set by his peers. The hair on the back of Zionée's neck tingled with disgust at the thought of this underachiever looking at her. When he caught her reflection looking, he returned her gaze through looking back at the window. She looked away for a moment to return her attention to the lecture but she felt his eyes lingering on her. After she took another glance back, she found that Rigley was actually looking away. When he noticed her looking again, he turned back, expecting to meet her eyes with the reflection of his own. She was looking away. They continued echoing glances off the glass at each other countless times throughout class. Finally, she tightened her look into a hard scowl and turned to where he was actually sitting until he noticed her and turned his attention elsewhere. Satisfied, she went back to her reading.

In AP History class, there was another rumor going around about Tessa. Rigley threw an eraser up in the air to catch everybody's attention with something laterally interesting.

"So Mulan and Joan of Arc are in a bar and the barman –"

"Rigley, no one wants to know," said the history teacher.

"Why?"

"Try waiting for the sound of someone to ask," added Zionée. Both their teacher and classmates erupted with laughter.

Tessa sits down in class at her new favorite spot under the flickering ceiling light and starts to fill out a black and yellow meal-ticket application. She lies about her parent's income. Then she proceeds to write her socioeconomic status.

"Are you illiterate?"

She turns around and there is Derrion Yogun, with an airy look.

"What do you care?" making her voice sound low and boyish.

"For starters, you misspelled socioeconomic," says Derrion. "But I'm not talking about books."

He swipes Tessa's application off of her desk and gestures to turn it in for her.

"Listen, white boy. You got balls. More than the rest around here, anyways. If you interested in a little politics, under my wing is where you should fly."

"And where would I fly?"

"Above their reach, for starters," Yogun gestures at the injured bullies who are now picking on a bespectacled kid.

"I'm not afraid of them."

"The reach of their words is what I mean, brother. It doesn't take a lot to wind you up, huh? With your bony fists, I can see you running out of weapons some day and then looking for an inventory upgrade. One that I've seen too many become part of the price they pay for."

"I don't need a lecture on quid pro quo," Tessa says, folding her meal tickets. "And I'm not that kind of psychopath. What's it to you, anyways?"

"When I graduate this year, I'll need someone to succeed me around here."

Tessa raises her eyebrows.

"At being what? Class rep?"

He chuckles at her response before walking back to his seat.

Zionée stood before the ocean water, feeling every cold lick against her ankles. There was something more horrifying than being stranded forever on a Malibu beach. Something worse than losing her backpack or the fact that their first AP Chemistry review quiz was tomorrow and that she had no means of taking it on time. Almost as terrifying as how Rigley was just swimming back to shore and how badly she wanted to drown him before he reached the sand. She was actually scared for one moment into asking herself what Tessa Seredin would have done. The foamy water continued to pull light into her reflection's increasing ghost. She glanced upwards at the horizon again. Rigley was finding his way back to the sandy edge, awkward like the first life to come out of the ocean. As he made his way towards her, his silhouette was shiny, and he quickly rubbed his hands to his chest to warm up. She fought down the urge to drown him as he rose away from the water still deep enough to do so.

It was sabotage.

Rigley had been placed on Zionée's team. His GPA was so low that it brought their team average down like an anchor stopping the course of the grand and powerful ship that was her academic ambition. Subsequently, they were labeled Team Omega. Earlier that evening, both Zionée and Edin were locked in respective bathroom stalls by poisoned cupcakes and hinges bolted to the wrong side of the door. After finally kicking their way out, it was too late. After finding out that everyone had disappeared with the bus, they began searching at where the sand stopped being wet. Their old backpacks, which contained their cell phones, could not be found.

The air was aural with the massive roar of the ocean. Far out in the darkening horizon, new lights were born before the stars, motionless but winking: boats and buoys, floating on the misty horizon of the tidally calm sea. But soon a choir of distant, roaring waves joined the tidal symphony rolling under the changing tempo of the lunar conductor. All but the gulls evacuated the face of the entire beach, which was now freckled fully with the many depressions of faded footprints. There was a fresh, red pail by the far edge of the shore left, Zionée presumed, by some child collecting material to make a sand castle with his mother and father; two lights of which must have shone brightly over his days, was now a reminding of the dark over her own.

They peered toward the sidewalk avenue lining the edge of the beach where there must have been someone at business with the world. All shops were closed. It was like some strange silent, holiday had begun without their knowing. They were quiet in the coldness.

Back at Sheltevue, Principal Flores greeted the last three kids coming off the bus at dusk, all looking old enough to be in college. The two dark-haired boys had typically handsome features and the girl was sandy blonde with a makeup-enhanced face.

"And who are you three supposed to be?"

"I'm Rig…"

"A little too prepared to introduce yourselves for someone you're not," Flores said, her voice trembling with a power unfamiliar the other students. "You're not Rigley. You're not… you know what, why don't you pronounce your name for me?"

"My name. Right, my name is… Zye-yonee?"

Flores laughed a little hysterically. The other kids instinctively frowned, sensing the descent of her wrath tightening the very air in their lungs.

"Right, thought so," she said, taking out her walkie-talkie.

"Look lady, you don't have to get the cops, okay?"

It wasn't dark enough for Flores to not see the rings around their eyes and she also noticed the particular way that the air around them stung.

"I don't know. Is my nose going to help me decide or your cooperation?"

"We're from Malibu State."

As soon as she saw Team Alpha snickering at the back seat, she pointed her finger at them, gesturing them to stay there and wait for their punishment. Then she told the senile, old chauffeur to lead the rest of the class to the entrance gates where their parents waited.

"Malibu State," Flores said to herself as she took out her cell phone. "Hey, Vicky?"

"Hi, Flores!" came a jolly voice through the phone.

"Don't you have a sports meet today?"

"Water tennis!" she screamed.

"Okay," said Flores, wincing. "Great. Where at?"

"Oh, is this about not showing up to the auditorium meeting yesterday to meet my team? I am so sorry, Flores. I was reading up for..."

"Hey, you're not under my jurisdiction anymore, I won't ask you what you read. But if you happen to be by Malibu State, do you remember the route to the Hourglass Beach?"

"Oh the start of the year field trip? Yeah. I love that place."

"Great, well you've got a chance at making up for not showing up to the auditorium meeting."

"Oh, really? Awesome! Thanks, Flores."

"No, wait – don't hang up!"

Flores sighed as she got ready to re-dial but the phone rang by itself. She placed it to her ear while glowering at the three students she had still yet to punish sitting idly in the back of the bus.

"Ha, sorry, Flores. I'm playing flip cup."

"You're kidding!" Flores's voice cracked slightly. "Vicky, I need you sober!"

"Chill to the nth power, Flores. Do you know how good I am at this game?"

"Don't make me assume."

"What do you need me for?"

"To steal a bus and rescue your team from that beach so they can avoid showing up late for their first day of school!"

She had flowing, dark hair with large, clef note earrings and was of Indian and Hawaiian descent. Running to the parking lot where the sports team buses were, Vicky quickly went and retrieved her things. Then she put on her orange jump suit and checked her backpack. She cracked her neck with an athletic eloquence and took out a few books and some reading lights.

"Okay, Team Omega! I'm on my way," Vicky said.

She snuck on to a bus and started the engine, waving out the window at the rival sports team she had competed against that day. Ronna, the pretty Asian-American leader of Team Alpha pointed at the vehicle she and her teammates were about to get on.

"Hey, isn't that our bus?"

They quickly unsheathed their rackets and ran after it but it had already started moving away. By the time Vicky got there, they were like three cold phantoms haunting the vacant sidewalk by the entrance to the beach. A single blade of fluorescence, angled down at the bench they stood next to, divided their shadows from their silhouettes. As she quickly got them onto the bus with the heater on at full blast, Vicky had a look of sleepy bemusement for their distinct eccentricities of accent, age, and attitude. Upon noticing how far back they sat, she turned off the engine.

"What are you doing?" Zionée protested.

"I'm not moving," Vicky said cheekily.

"Why?"

"A stranger drives up to you with a bus and all three of you get on without a word. Boy, have I got a lot to teach you."

"We figured out who you are."

"So is it faith in someone that makes you so smart or are you just being a bitch?"

Rigley gasped and almost laughed until he saw how serious and still Zionée became.

"Relax, I was just kidding around with you," Vicky quickly added guiltily with her eyes closed in a comedic fashion. "Sorry, okay?"

Edin, who was almost asleep, got up and took a seat in the isle directly behind her. Rigley and Zionée followed, sitting far apart from each other on opposite isles.

"That's better," Vicky smiled. "See? It's important to get to know people. It's how you tell apart the psychos from the friends. And even when you can't, you can still learn to rely on them."

"Learning fast," said Rigley.

"It's because I still look your age, huh? I'm actually a sophomore again."

"Aren't most of the Team Counselors only freshman?"

"AP credit," she said, pointing at the characters on the flap of Zionée's mantle flap. "Such as Japanese. Shione?"

"Zionée."

"Oh right, that character becomes "Zi" with the apostrophe things," Vicky chuckled. "My bad."

Vicky turned to the boyish face with the bright, big eyes.

"And you are?"

"He's Edin," said Zionée.

"Okay. I'll take your big sister's word for it," said Vicky with a puckering, sarcastic tone as she turned the heater up. "Well, whatever we are, warm is one thing we're not."

Edin started to write in his notebook when his eraser rolled off and fell onto the floor of the bus. As he reached down in the dark to feel for it, Vicky started driving and it rolled further off. He was unable to find it and became anxious about the now limited ways to hide the doodle on his page from his sister. When he felt someone poking his shoulder he turned around slowly. It was Rigley who handed him his eraser.

"Thanks," Edin mouthed. Almost sure that he was too quiet for Rigley to hear, he was stunned to see him nod.

Zionée clicked on her penlight and tucked it behind an ear to continue writing down from memory all of the chapter's formulas she studied for. After a while, she noticed Rigley looking past her and out through her window. The extra notebooks and pencils Vicky had given them rested idly on his seat.

"Hey, you should probably copy these down to study," said Zionée. "I mean if I were you, I'd be... Actually, I don't know what I would do if I were you."

"You could try waiting for the sound of someone to ask," Rigley said with his tongue between his teeth.

She tried to ignore his humming but soon realized he had stopped a while ago and that it was coming from somewhere else. The satellite radio picked up a Japanese pop station. The daylight hatched across the sky like a pale, gold yolk slowly frying on a wide, endless pan. The smell of the salted soul of the ocean was finally gone and in its place was the smoky ghost of air conditioner heat lingering off the leather seats. As the bright edge of the horizon flared beyond the windows, she could now see that his eyes were as brown as clearly as he could see that her own were green. Zionée grabbed her notepad and leapt across the isle to sit next to him. Together they began studying for the test that they were expected to miss. Zionée stared out the window glass for a moment as the notes of the Japanese Rock beat started to paint the lines into what became Rigley's translucent reflection, astonishing her with something she had never seen him do before in class: working hard. Edin, holding the eraser, gently brushed the miniscule, rubbery shavings off the pad and modified his drawing of three stick figures and their new team leader.

1st SEMESTER

2 – Team Ranking System

On one Sunday afternoon, before the ceremonial start-of-the-year field trip to the Hourglass Beach, the students were gathered in the auditorium for an important meeting. Behind the crimson curtains, Principal Flores was haphazardly doodling in her last-minute speech on the back of some flash cards from old homework assignments. Professor Nairs of the History department tapped the microphone on the podium to quiet the crowd. Nairs was wearing her usual, casual attire with her Indian complexion complimenting the brown shemagh she had confiscated from a drama student a while ago. Her dark hair was combed back and kept down by a bow. Finally having shuffled the cards in the right order, Flores walked through the curtains and signaled for a louder silence. The wide, cavernous theater full of young silhouettes was a little unsettling. She could hear them shifting in their seats and turning their unseen gazes towards her.

"Good afternoon, students and parents of Sheltevue Gifted," she began, her South American accent travelling far across the acoustic space. "I want to start by..." Flores squinted a little at her own writing, which had been scribbled too fast to be legible.

"Team Ranking System!" she declared, dropping the card down. "Imagine sitting in the back of the class all the time, barely raising your hand when your teachers have questions. You're a B-student, C-student, or a D – whatever. And you know that if you just put in those extra hours you could be that confident A-student sitting in the heart of the classroom. But you don't. Right? Perhaps it is because you feel unmotivated, discouraged, and even insulted by those A-students."

The crowd was quiet.

"But not always by their intelligence," she paused. "By their success."

The lighting seemed to narrow around her like she was doing stand-up comedy, forcing all other shapes in the auditorium to fall stealthily into the dark. She wiped some perspiration from her eyebrows and continued.

"I've been a student under every one of those alphabetic labels and I can tell you, at every level, the feeling is there. How do I fight off the fear and intimidation I feel from somebody who I think is better than me?"

"Take it outside of class!" one student shouted. There was a ripple of laughter. And not without the whine of the boy who got his ears pulled by his parents.

Flores sighed.

"Yeah. I can do that. That's one suggestion. Not a good one. A step in the right direction towards that infamous early kind of graduation we call expulsion. But it is also a choice that reflects how one can lose the battle to fear. Compete. Don't give up. And understand that equality isn't default. It isn't something handed to you. You have to fight for it. In doing so, you'll start to understand others who aren't the same as you."

Not far past the first couple of rows, she could see the sports watches glittering in the dark from parents checking the time. Some of the students were beginning to yawn and shut their eyes. Flores almost dropped her flash cards until she imagined the eyes of her one friend staring back from the middle of the front row. She hadn't come that day.

After slipping on the mash potatoes, a couple teachers walked by and stared down at her while the entire room rippled with the politest possible laughter anyone could manage.

"So what else is on the syllabus this year?" asked an African-American English teacher who tried hard to suppress a laugh. Professor Tammy had almost shoulder-length dreadlocks and wore stylish, frameless glasses. At her table, Professor Nairs quickly put her phone away but Flores could tell she was going to publish the results of her humiliation just as she had published theirs.

"Nice eyeliner. Is it for the art department?" laughed Professor Esparanza, the Asian-American AP Spanish teacher. She was a tall, dark-haired woman with sharp, flat eyes. The Australian science teacher walked over with a soda and decided to join in. Professor Weavins's sarcastic eyebrows were arched so high at that the skin on his forehead smiled symmetrically to his condescending frown. He tried to hide his receding hairline by shaping it into a widow's peak. Weavins was not only one of the hardest graders but also one of the harshest comedians. Flores almost froze with shame and humiliation as more of them gathered around her. Suddenly, she was blanketed by the shadow of the big ponytail of a girl who was wearing a custom sailor uniform. She was standing in front of her and held out what looked like her eyeliner. Her face started to cool.

"I think it's a great eyeliner," she said. "You should all try it. It really brings the spite out of your eyes."

Esparanza exchanged looks with the others before breaking out in much less restrained laughter. Flores noticed the hand holding the eyeliner start to shake a little bit. She suddenly bolted up on her feet, not caring anymore about the bright, red-orange sauce on her purple jacket.

"Stop laughing at her! All of you can laugh at me but the next time someone falls down at this school, no matter where they are, I expect you to act like the people you're paid to be. Or there will be parking permits confiscated. Understood?"

Professors Tammy and Esparanza became silent and gestured for their T.A's to follow them back to their table. Weavins scoffed and went to the soda machine again.

"Thanks," said Flores, taking the eyeliner pen from her before noticing it was coated in chocolate.

"Sorry," Zionée said. "I used it up."

Flores slightly gasped when she took a good look at her hard face for the first time to see the tarantula-esque flowers hiding two brilliant emeralds. Back at the auditorium, she coughed a little to hide the small laugh escaping with the thought of how they met.

"That's what the Team Ranking System is going to be about. You choose a team of three people, classmates I hope who are not just your friends, and you will average together your scores into one Team GPA," she said over the collecting wails of disapproval from both students and parents alike.

"At the end of the year, the team with the Highest GPA average –"

Flores hesitated.

She could hear the creaking of the foldout seats. Their young minds were already brewing with ideas of supremacy behind their glistening eyes. A scholarship grant to the prestigious college of their choice was but the icing. The ability to justify their might over their competing classmates would be trophy enough. Among the large audience, there was a growing restlessness and noise of chatter.

"Well I hope you get the idea. If not now, then eventually when you're carrying the weight of someone else's pride other than your own. Somewhere down the year, maybe you can all learn something meaningful about each other."

Professor Nairs tapped her wristwatch from offstage and Flores picked up her cards from the podium and shuffled ahead to the last one.

"Now today, again, I want to thank you all for bringing your parents but most importantly each other. Since the online announcement of the teams, you have all been assigned one Team Counselor volunteering from a prestigious college you've all had a dream or two, I'm sure, of getting into. Today, at the back of the stage, you will meet them and exchange contacts and form a bond of teacher and student that will hopefully stay with you throughout the year. Snacks and drinks have been made available, of course."

With that came the obligatory applause. Flores looked down at her unread cards and smiled disappointedly at the points she did not get to make. As she walked around the auditorium a while later, she grew bored from talking to parents and noticed Edin reading alone at the edge of a prop table on the stage.

"Hello Edin," Flores said, sitting down across from him.

Edin nodded and put the book down. His eyes were still tattooed with dictionary words most students his age did not know how to look up.

"Your TC wasn't able to show up today, huh? I'll make sure she does soon. She had a water tennis meet."

Edin raised his eyebrow but didn't remove his gaze from the book.

"I know, weird school huh? Oh but it's a really good one too."

Flores followed the direction of his gaze to a portly man in his forties and an Asian-American trophy wife.

"Those are the new fosters, huh? Are they nice?"

He remained still for a long time before finally shrugging.

"And your sister?"

Edin shook his head and used a hand to demonstrate the motion of running and kicking.

"Oh right, she has a game."

Flores moved a hand to her ear and wrinkled the corner of her mouth with a half-smile before taking out her computer tablet. Although they often had a lot of fun cracking jokes about the trivial details of the day, she was aware that her top student was never so amiable around her peers. In Zionée's eyes, her classmates were literally children and it scared Flores to think if this was because of her intellect or her self-obliged sense of maturity. As she started opening the online records for Team Omega, Flores looked over their individual grades and looked at Edin.

"Not bad, so far. Think you can average on to that 4.0 till sophomore year?"

He nodded again.

"And now let's see, Zionée of course… perfect. So let's see if… she's ever going to talk to me again," Flores joked, smiling at Edin, who half-smiled back after learning from the way she did it a few minutes ago.

"Rigley's grades. Here they are. A lot of B's… oh and C's… Some "U" marks for unsatisfactory. Well, there's room."

Flores grimaced at what she saw for the first term of his freshman year.

"Holy Humpty Dumpty," she said. "Now it totally makes sense why your team is starting off at the bottom."

Edin shrugged and she looked him in the eye.

"So what about you, personally? Do you want to win the scholarship?"

Edin gestured with his hand as if to say something more complex than he could manage with a nod or shake of his head.

"Hey Flores, when did you learn sign language?" asked Professor Weavins, who was wearing a New Zealander dress shirt even though Flores had told all of the teachers to dress formally for this one particular day.

"Piss off Weavins, it's not a learning disability."

"Good, then I can mark him down when he doesn't speak."

As Weavins walked back to the other teachers, Edin glowered in his direction. Flores turned back to him and softly smiled before putting her tablet back in her backpack. He blinked at her as she got up to go discuss other school plans with the staff, finding her a little peculiar but less so than why his sister would come to trust an adult so fast.

Although their real parents left them when they were too young to remember, they both grew up quickly enough to distinguish their first foster parents apart from them. Zionée was always sharp and cunning and, even from a one-digit age, plotted to have them abandoned or put back up for adoption whenever they came into a conflict of interests with their current fosters. Edin knew that even if they were strangers as newborns, Zionée learned to walk before she could crawl. He struggled every day of his life to catch up to her. When Zionée joined her first sports team, he helped her practice. It did not matter that he initially didn't know how to play soccer; it was an obligation, automatic of his love for his one real family, to learn all that he could about the rules. When Zionée started one of her clubs, he took to managing the first day of it so that he could see and collect data on all who had shown up. When Zionée did community service at the library, he also clocked hours in by helping the P.E. teachers put away the equipment. He was always in the shadow of her learning curve and wanted to know all she had to endure, all the hard turns and chinks in her self-esteem, and all the small but rewarding thrills of becoming a little better than when first starting out. It gave their lives a routine momentum.

After studying in his room for five hours, he closed the chemistry book and patted the cover gently with his hand as if pacifying a pet animal. He took out the newspaper article of Tessa Seredin and looked at the picture again. Then he looked at the eyes on his own reflection in the bedroom window. When he heard Zionée come in shortly after knocking on the door, he quickly shoved the article back inside of the drawer. Later in the bathroom, he breathed over the mirror to create enough condensation to smear clear the two holes where his reflection's eyes would be. Tessa's eyes seemed more real when Zionée's reflection was in the glass. Sharp and slightly slanted like almond. His eyes appeared flat and quite horizontal. The bathroom light showed a gray-bluish tint and in no iridescent angle did it ever come to appear green. But if there was any hope that he might have, any spark of himself in Tessa, it was the photograph. It was aged and taken in black-and-white. He consoled himself with the possibility that he might have had more of the father's genes. But there were no articles he could find about a Mr. Seredin or any indication as to whether Seredin was even a surname carried over by marriage.

As the school year started, Edin thought about his conversation with Principal Flores a few days after the field trip incident. When they were at the beach, he learned that people were not kind. They were most vicious when they pretended to be.

"Hi Zionée," said Carrie, the tanned, freckly girl walking up to them with a basket of cupcakes. "I baked these."

"Nice."

"I didn't want you to feel left out," she said, holding out the basket to optimize the reach of its alluring blueberry fumes. "Everybody already had one."

"Sweet of you."

"Maybe too?"

"Why would you ask?"

"Assuming that you would."

"I wouldn't," Zionée said wearily.

"Is this your brother? He's so cute. I see him managing your clubs all the time."

"He's much older than he looks."

Carrie handed Edin a cupcake. Zionée sighed and took one too. She stood in their way as they tried to continue moving. The sand lightened under their feet.

"You that self-conscious of a cook?"

Carrie smiled bitterly and grabbed the cupcake from Edin but Zionée grabbed it and returned it to his hand.

"No, it's okay. Edin, be polite with me. My classmate worked very hard on this, I'm sure."

Edin was suspicious of the look on Carrie's face when she lingered to watch them finish it. The curl of her lips and the brief inanimate stillness of her should have told him that she was suspending her breath in anticipation of something awful.

In class, Edin watched the trees outside the window. The wind increased the agility of the silhouetted canopy, which projected against the walls a spinning pattern of light like a fast, botanic zoetrope.

Out on the campus grounds, people were leading lives in metronome with their distinct social groups. His absence among them was the surest sign that he was in school. Someone who, even when he spoke aloud, nobody could hear what sense it was he made. Every day at the beginning of lunch, Rigley would unpack the exotic smell of his mother's cooking in empty classrooms. He ate quietly while listening to music by setting his earphones inside a seashell at full volume so that the acoustics would magnify the sound from a tangible, almost living object. At the beginning of time, like the first creature to appear, alive and alien unto itself, he was alone. Once and a while he would see Edin walk past the usually open door. But he often imagined it because of the way the wind sung through the shaking trees by rattling its branches and leaves.

Rigley finished his food and wiped his mouth with some napkins. Then he took out a thick, permanent marker. He started tagging under the tables of the classmates he didn't like. After sweeping the whole room, he quickly stuck his head out the door. No one was there. He chucked the faded marker off of the second floor balcony of the history building. Under each of the desks, unbeknownst to most of his classmates, were bubblegum calendars. He'd stick a gum under the date and then, depending on how differently he had been treated by the person out of whatever mood they were in that day, foul or pleasant, he'd write an insult or leave it alone. Rigley took out one more piece of gum, chewed it, and stuck a piece under his own desk.

As he walked down the hallway with a black and green backpack that was light enough to not affect his posture, carrying most of his heavy books in one hand, he looked them knowingly in the eyes as they passed by, day-to-day, from varying social distances. Inside many of them he could see a capacity for evil and wickedness, which for some was infinitely masked behind pretty faces and friendly facades, all the while subscribed to an interior network of wit and cruelty. In the constant indecision of morality that was adolescence, Rigley was in a space to be decisive because he was alone.

He arrived a few minutes late to AP European History and sat down at a table surrounded by his classmates. Like him, some of them were culturally accented in a way that strongly contradicted how they appeared on the outside. But despite this sometimes-instinctive sense of being mutual outcasts, it did not keep him from being ostracized.

"Move off, Rigley. That's my seat," said a curly-haired boy with a large shirt as he arrived to class. Edmondo usually had a bored tone of irritation when he spoke to Rigley. He was of some Filipino descent but grew up mostly in Mexico. As one of the highest grades in the class, he was friendliest to those who were the smartest at a subject and didn't ask stupid questions. When Rigley was introducing himself to everybody, Edmondo was one of the first to acknowledge him and greet him. But he did not anticipate how prone to mistakes in humor and learning he would be. Hashim, a passive boy of Indian heritage but with a Canadian accent and preppy dress sense, chuckled. Though Hashim was friendly enough to lend Rigley his history textbook one class period ago, he did not hesitate to laugh at him under the alchemy of different company. Edmondo was his best friend and although he didn't mind Rigley's faulty and often senseless humor, he was quick to mishandle his loyalty in a sycophantic fashion.

"Don't be so mean, guys," said the German-accented Letitia,

who was of African descent and was sitting next to Rigley. The fashionably dressed Letitia was often using old, expired make-up kits as an art inventory for her elaborate class doodles, which outshined Rigley's pencil sketches.

"Yeah, sorry for loitering on your parking space," said Rigley, getting up from the chair roughly. "There's a permit for asswhipe somewhere here."

"Yeah, I'm sure you'll find it in your pocket, Rigley," Edmondo said.

"Oh, what a burn," said Letitia.

They laughed at him. In spite of this, Rigley hovered around them for a brief while but could find nothing to connect to their conversation. Soon, he could see his reflection in each of their irises evaporate like smoke. As he walked to find another seat, he could hear Zera's friendly voice.

"Yeah, so during flag football, Edmondo was being such a sore loser."

"Uh, and that girly way he perms his hair with that spray when he's nervous," said Debby. Zera's best friend was Debby. She had curly, blonde hair and frosty, green eyes. They were sitting near the center of the classroom so Rigley was confident that Edmondo could hear them.

"I know, right?" Zera laughed.

Rigley stood still, allowing his feelings to shut down before their words could reach him. But nonetheless, his mirror neurons fired off. Zera was supposed to be on Edmondo's team but she hasn't once spoken to them about it in class. She was Jewish-American with a little trace of English blood and often sported her blue track team hoodie. She had a perfect Middle American accent but had an airy ring to her speech because of her asthma. In a few desk rows away, she was laughing with her friends Debby and Rickward, in a gaudy and obnoxious way. Rickward had dark, brown hair and voids in his eyes. They had the charismatic gravity of beautiful people but dressed normally and not bombastically. A sedative symptom of their beauty was that no matter how mad they might have made someone, they could always make them forgive and forget. A beauty that was limited in its depth to skin alone with a world full of malice underneath. Rigley continued his way to the front of the class ignoring their glances as he passed. They were all already strangers again in moments discontinuous with how he was last treated by them.

Rigley was the academic runt of the privates and one of the two most unpopular class clowns. He had never met the other one. And unlike his classmate Cory, who hung around the Rickward and Debby but was also a poor student, he did not have the features of some ideal, pop worship. Under the patterns of tolerance set by all of his classmates and further validated by the favoritism their academic prowess drew out of their teachers, he was the easiest target to their criticism. In the daily competition of obnoxious egos, despite making enemies from their gossip and ridicule of each other, they all had one in common in Rigley. His grades scared them. His mistakes scared them. His constant messing up and embarrassing himself in front of the class terrified them. But worst of all it was his attitude towards it all that was what antagonized them the most.

Under the brightest ceiling light, Rigley reluctantly sat down in the seat closest to the teacher's desk. Upon realizing that this happened to be the seat next to his teammate, he turned around to see if there were any more empty seats. They were all taken. Zionée arrived and sat down in her now routinely audible body language. One by one, she slammed her books out of her backpack in common time before detaching the pencil case attached to her knee and slapping that onto the table in a neatly organized arrangement. Then she stared forward at the teacher's empty desk for what seemed like minutes without saying anything while the noise level faded around them. Weavins arrived late and handed back their chemistry review results. She looked at his score and then raised her eyes back at him. Her eyes slowly started to close but not completely. It was like she was chewing up the image of him with her fanged eyelids in a cold and despising squint.

"I looked at the chapter and I –," Rigley said seriously.

Zionée focused her attention on the textbook page, ignoring him. Rigley then occupied himself by watching the way the bright daylight multiplied the orange and yellow colors of autumn across the panes of the classroom. For a small moment, she looked up from her reading and noticed him at this.

On his way to lunch, Rigley moved down the main hallway

and saw Zionée standing in front of the large digital scoreboard that now had all of their Team Rankings listed up on it like destinations at an airport terminal. He started to notice that she always wore her sailor uniform but sometimes customized it with a collar or a hoodie. She was crunching a ball of paper in her fist and looking at the digital scroll of their team name. They were on the bottom of the list.

"Will you come with me?"

"To do what?" Rigley replied apathetically.

A freshman with a black eye gasped when his diaphragm intercepted her fist. He dropped his lunch bag into Zionée's hands and then ran off.

"To have lunch."

They sat by the flat, stone steps leading up to the back entrance of the main building. The huge, gothic building loomed over them with many windows glimmering in the sail of sunlight. At the top of the structure were the forever-closed eyes of the bell room. The school used an electronic one instead of the ancient instrument hidden inside behind those dusty, gray wooden lids.

"I need you to cheat off of me," she said a few moments later.

"What?"

He shook his head.

"I told you if we practiced the ways I've come up with – you wouldn't get caught."

Rigley looked down at his hands for a moment and shook his head.

"I've been caught at a lot of things," he said.

She stared at him angrily while he proceeded to eat the strange curry.

"Who was that kid by the way?"

"He's a freshman. And him and his dumbass friends were pushing kids around in Edin's class."

"But not Edin?"

"It was only a matter of time," she said, looking at him.

"How good of you."

"So," she said, finishing her sandwich crust, "you understand how we're going to do it?"

"Don't need to. Because I won't."

"And why the fuck not?"

Her eyes glowed with an emerald fire.

"Are you used to cussing?"

"With all the time I'm going to spend with you, I have a feeling I will be."

She crinkled the empty lunch bag in her hands while they sat in silence. Rigley took a sip of the bubble tea.

"Everyone cheats at one point or another."

"Not me."

"That's B.S! I would too if I needed to."

"I'm not sure you mean that," he began.

The skin around Zionée's eyes tightened and her mouth opened with surprise. She took the bubble tea from his hands.

"Sorry, did you want that?"

"That was from MY lunch!"

Rigley looked away and she couldn't tell if he was embarrassed or snickering.

"Whatever, look, I need you to do this for the team."

"I don't need a handicap, okay?" Rigley said, defiant and passionate but not angry.

"Yes, you do!"

Zionée clenched her fingers into the flesh of her black and blue backpack with growing frustration.

"No! If you –," Rigley stopped, trying hard not to let the fuse of her temper light his own so that he could continue to make his point without getting defensive.

"If I what?" Zionée demanded.

"Gave me a chance to prove that I don't have to betray my own smarts, my own potential, just so you can fake our way up to the top."

"Oh and being lazy and procrastinating isn't considered a betrayal of that potential?"

"You got me there," Rigley said, looking at her impressed but humiliated. "But that is something I can work on."

"There's more at stake to me than just your stupid moral dilemma, " she said, her thin nostrils flaring.

"You're right. Yours. Because riding on a lie as a way up to success is just... conceit."

"I'm not conceited," Zionée said defensively. He moved a

hand through his somewhat messy hair and she touched a lace of her shoes. In spite of how, like most people, they didn't maintain eye contact from the awkwardness of it, she nonetheless waited to hear what he had to say next while pretending to have something more interesting on her mind.

"And I'm saying you don't have to be. Just like I don't have to cheat. If you were on a sports team, would you make your teammates take steroids?"

Zionée bit her tongue.

"I want this," she said, sucking on her tongue and relieved that there was no sharp, metallic taste but she knew that it was going to be sore for a few days. "It's important to me. I have to be on the top of that chart."

She scratched her nose and shook her head. Rigley was a little surprised by the sincerity and desperation in her slightly dehydrated voice.

"So satisfying your ego is more important than the integrity of our team?"

Zionée tisked. He didn't know what ego meant to someone who had so much going for it. The risk of failure to her was an epic and unfamiliar chasm. It was not an incidental disappointment but a threat to the mortality of her self-image.

"I'm telling you, if we did this, we wouldn't be the only ones cheating."

Rigley's eyes were intense and unblinking. Zionée looked and felt drawn into them but tried to fight away. As soon as she realized she had just memorized the color of his eyes, she knew that she was losing.

"I would rather be the ones who don't," he continued. "I know that I'm a rubbish student. And I've never been on a team before so if this is how it works, then I'll learn what's my weight to pull."

The sky was blue with not a cloud in sight to threaten the clarity of it. Although they continued holding eye contact with one another, Rigley could hear her hand move down to her ankle and the snap of plastic. They both looked away for a moment to stare into the wide and noisy wilderness of the campus courtyard, populated with more strangers than friends. Although the campus was mostly full of teenagers, the distance of their disperse transformed them into sounding like children. But the collective chatter in the background was now an island away. They could almost hear the waves and winds of the ocean again. As though some mysterious and forgotten part of them was buried away with their old backpacks on the shores of that beach. But the rattling tree branches woke them up to where they were. Zionée turned to look at him again. He looked back and they both waited with their mouths closed. She opened her mouth for a moment to speak but then closed it again before standing up.

"Keep your stupid integrity!"

She started to walk off towards the large, wooden doors of the main building but stopped. Leaning down on one side, she opened a little pencil box strapped above her left ankle and removed two sticks of Pocky. Looking as though she had forgotten why she took out a second one, she turned around, with one stick in her mouth, and awkwardly handed it to Rigley and mouthing "here" before storming off. He looked at the stick of Pocky before holding it close to his nose.

From inside the first floor hallway, Zionée was watching him near the electric chandelier by the doorway. She took out the remaining stick of chocolate and took a bite from it, not caring at first for the unusual flavor. He got up and walked towards her and she stopped trying to hide her smile of confident triumph. But the taste of it got stranger by the second.

"How's the eyeliner taste?"

She spat it out immediately without even looking at him and sprinted to the nearest water fountain to rinse repeatedly.

3 – The Literacy of Pain

Tessa wipes the crimson drool from her newly bruised mouth. She rubs one sore, black eye with some alcoholic cotton. It aches with the reminding sting to never let her guard down there again. Then she sighs with a little difficulty from the pain in her abdomen and chest. The emotional injustices of the latest fight continue to run through her mind as she sits in class. It is always another yesterday. She starts tapping her pencil against the weathered desktop. The clicks of lead against wood are in the same signature as the teacher's monotone delivery. A couple of desks away, she overhears a girl with greased back hair and her dark, blonde friend talking.

"Yeah, did you know that Cassie's brother is actually her... you know?"

"What? No way! I could not tell."

"I hear she wraps her chest up with sports tape."

Tessa's eyes are alert. She starts taking mental notes.

"Girl, she's only between an A and B cup anyway."

She looks down briefly at her androgynous armor of blue denim. With not a single P.E class throughout the year, she can stay in the same costume all throughout the days.

"You got some mascara looking eyes there, white boy," says Mason, a large, weighty classmate with oily skin in a faded, gray shirt. "Chill, I'm just kidding with you."

In class, they get assigned to work in groups. First, Tessa gets a compliment from a girl for a remark she makes. The girl giggles. Mason doesn't laugh at this. A few moments later, she hears about how people think she wears mascara. Soon, it seems like everybody starts talking trash about the feminine features of her face. Mason turns to her and sees the family tree on her desk.

"Fool, you done yet?"

As he continues talking, the cold, sinking feeling in her heart starts to grow. His friendliness starts to change and slip off like the skin of some snake.

"You call that a tree? Where's your mom? Huh? You'll get marked off for incomplete."

He takes the tree chart from her desk and a while later, the girls in the nearby table giggles. Some of the guys laugh too. The clock ticks but doesn't appear to move. The pulse of Tessa's heart grows louder. He turns to her again with another twisted smear of a smirk. The teacher sits in the back as still as furniture. She ignores his taunts. The kid turns around and continues talking to the others. She starts hearing them talk about her mother. Tessa clenches her pencil until the wood snaps. He turns to her and pretends to be all friendly again. But she now sees the drawing he is showing to the others on her tree chart. It is vulgar and evil and causes the percussion in her to pick up a faster tempo. She hears him saying with his back turned to her that she hates herself because her mother hated queers. He is stepping on her wounds: first he made fun of her race and then her sexuality and then her family members. Their classmates are now noisy and shouting, adding their own arrangements. All of them laugh fiendishly, orchestrated to the fire burning in their hearts from each their own insecurity. He turns to her and laughs. She pulls her lips in and breathes through her nose.

"Oh yeah, look at your bitch-ass eyes getting red. No wonder you wear mascara."

He slaps the hat off the top of Tessa's head. The back of her neck is now too hot, stopping the blood needed to think straight from reaching her brain. The air is palpable with the raw sting of her injury. Her hands tighten. She flexes her bruised knuckles.

"Ay, is this your mom?"

He points at the crude, vulgar drawing of a stick figure on her tree chart. The sick laughter of the others pollutes her ears.

"Hey, man it's cool. I'll turn it in for you."

The teacher is already making his way.

"Hey, fool. You should watch out for some of these hypocrites. They'll talk a lot of shit behind your back."

More laughter rings in her ears.

"Hey, is this your mom?"

Suddenly the metallic legs of the desk violently slide against the floor. Tessa's fist swings fast but one of his cronies catches her wrist so she uses the other arm to punch him out of the way. The other kids start hollering and cheering off of the amplitude of their hate. She strikes the bully's jaw fast, optimizing her message across the nerves leading back to that sick and miserable mind of his. Blood and bruises form from the flesh craters of her bare-knuckled impact. Before she can go too far, the science teacher intercepts her wrist and she socks him without meaning to. He doubles over in pain. Many students around them gasp and become silent. Then Tessa throws her fist back at its original destination. The kid feels another smash of her knuckles sooner than he can blink. Yogun, from across the classroom, looks up and watches the same, familiar daydream unfold.

"Yogun," Alonzo nudges him. "The kid should be getting floored. Can't he just be bullied in peace? Mason messes with every new kid."

Yogun looks at him and yawns.

"Mason is just a local predator," Yogun says. "Ain't got much imagination for being a man without making others feel like less of one."

Alonzo laughs as the mayhem spirals safely out of their way. The toughest of the public crowd do not have to go out of their way to intimidate others. They measure the value of others based on the way they hold themselves up against constant physical adversity. Yogun only associates himself with people who had the ability to outlast the wounds that contaminated their self-respect. Those who didn't, turned into bullies that feed off of others to find shelter from the sting of their own injustices, whether they learn to feel tough that way or because it's just the easiest sense of humor to adapt to. But he notices that there is something unusual about the way this kid survives his fights. A few seconds ago, Tessa is cursing at the top of his lungs with the foulest, most hateful language as though possessed. Now that the cops are here and the situation is defused, his abrupt stillness is eerie. After they cuff him again, the police lead him down the hall to the dean's office. Tessa is strangely cool. The wet light in her eyes catches the glare of the hallway chandelier and for a moment her pupils seem to disappear.

"Third time this week, kid," says the dean. "You trying to set a world record for quickest expulsion?"

Tessa stares on, bleeding and inattentive, but the man carries on the conversation with the window. He is wearing a formal dress shirt but also jeans. His voice carries the hollowness of someone who screams a lot with fascistic energy.

"You lost. Nephew of mine brought a gun to school," he says calmly, "Day one, freshman year. End of story. Zero tolerance."

"Is zero some kind of a variable?" she begins slowly. "You know. Like Algebra?"

"Excuse me?"

"It gets easy, doesn't it? After a while, turning your back."

With a balding cap of a head and beady eyes, the dean laughs a little bit before turning around with a serious and threatening look.

"Look, you piece of shit," he says. "This is not about dignity. Or respect. It's about rules. I don't care if your complete evolutionary line of existence has been insulted. Do the one thing that gets you out clean. Tell on someone. Or don't tell anyone at all. Just take it if you want to keep your pride so badly. Maybe invest in a shrink."

Tessa stares at him with a mix of disgust and horror.

"But what about you, huh?" he continues mockingly. "You're telling yourself that your violence is going to solve anything?"

"It won't."

"Are you being funny?"

She stands up and faces the door and considers giving him the finger as she turns around to face him one more time.

"Hey! Sit down!"

Instead she bites her lower lip but winces a little when she remembers it is still healing. Her voice is cool but steady.

"I'm not afraid of you. I can see the chains of society around your neck and I can see that you're a hypocrite but not that stupid to be so quick of one."

"That's it, you're out of here," he growls, writing frantically on a probation notice that he tears so fast he doesn't care about the paper cut on his finger.

"I'm not saying it's right or that it's wrong. But if those are the only two answers you're ever going to settle with then you're going to make a lot of mistakes."

"At what?"

"The question you never cared to ask. How do I come to school everyday to even have the privilege of worrying about my education or complain about my homework without somebody busting my balls every two minutes or threatening to beat me up? And don't you ever tell me what I tell myself. It may not be right, what many of us have to do to survive. But do you have any notion of how pathetic and shameful it feels? To have to duck and flinch and to hurt while you look like a fool? Every punch we throw is another attempt to seize control and keep us from the scariest thing in the world: looking stupid in front of them. Hey, at least these mistakes are teaching us something. And maybe you didn't get it right the first time around either."

The dean drops his mouth and is speechless. Tessa pulls her Italian immigrant hat low over her hairline to cast a shadow over her eyes. The man crumples up the write-up letter.

"If we don't defend the love that makes us who we are," she sighs. "There's nothing else we got here."

"Oh yeah?" the dean challenged in a cold, unsympathetic voice. "What if doing so makes you into something worse than what you were defending it from in the first place?"

"Then I just become another victim of this world," Tessa says in an almost resigned voice. "Like the rest of them. And hate myself the rest of my life bullying something weaker than me to feel strong."

He picks up the accusatory tone in her voice. She gets up and starts to walk toward the doorway.

"Hold it," he says. "That question you said I don't care to... I did. Sometimes I do still."

He holds a picture frame on his desk before putting it facedown so she can't see it.

"A kid?"

"Same stories as me."

"How much the same?"

He rubs at his wrists and then looks down and shakes his head. Then he looks up and glares at her while she hears him crumple the probation note.

"My probation?"

"This is the public, kid," the dean scoffs. "There are no vacations."

She looks down for a moment and then walks out the door, closing it with a loud thud. Before the echo can finish ringing, she hears somebody clapping.

"You past the test," Yogun says, who is waiting in the hallway.

"That's a first," she says.

He grins and nods to the hallway path. Alonzo rubs his nose before flipping her off. As they walk down the corridors of the public sector, she notices the darkening hues of graffiti growing bolder on the walls: a messy cascade of purple, green, and blue. A couple of privates walk past them like ghosts, not seeing them as though they are too, laughing about some obscure song they read for music class. They float off with nice clothes and heavy books to ivory halls full of polished glass and lockers with not a spot of gum or tagging. Tessa gives one good look at them as they trail off the corner of her scowl before turning away. On the other side of their dream is somebody else's nightmare.

In English class, Rigley was walking back to his desk after opening the windows for the teacher, who went outside to take some aspirin. Then he approached Debby's desk after overhearing something.

"Yeah?" she said.

"Is it true your boyfriend found Tessa Seredin's yearbook in a locker?"

"Is it any of your business if he did?"

He stared at her until she grimaced and looked away to continue her conversation with Zera. Not too annoyed, he grabbed the backpack off of the desk next to her.

"Hey!"

As Rickward was usually doing this kind of sport with the smaller valuables of other classmates he didn't like, it wasn't hard for Rigley to find people to throw it back and forth at while he struggled to intercept it. He threw the backpack at Edmondo who tossed it at Hashim. They continued throwing it around each other until Rickward came back. Then they threw it back and forth over his head as he reached for it. Cory laughed but didn't join in. Finally, Rickward punched Rigley in the stomach and grabbed his backpack. Rigley gasped with more surprise than pain but smiled as he could see he wounded up him up, hoping that he might have put him in a place to see how he's treated others. Professor Tammy came back to class and stared at her aspirin bottle to see if it was working.

"Rigley was throwing my backpack around."

"I wasn't asking," Tammy snapped.

"She sees it as it is and as you are, I feel plenty sorry for her," Rigley said, still recollecting the air in his voice. The class laughed.

"Very good, Rigley. You want to try it sometime?"

"Sure, Tammy."

"See this chalkboard? You will be cleaning it. Until I see it. As it was."

When Rigley returned to his seat with a heavy sigh, Zionée was shocked to see the square book-shape bulge behind his sweatshirt.

"I've been… working out."

Zionée made a sound like a gasp but wrestled the corner of her mouth with great effort, coughing a little and clearing her throat. She felt the eyes on his reflection in the window move to her.

Later in the school library, Edin arrived and placed a bottle of soup next to his sister. The lights in the lounge were economically distributed to mesh with what little daylight remained. Rigley pulled a seat out for Edin while Zionée continued to silently scribble and highlight.

"You don't want to look at it?" he asked her.

"Have you finished your preparations for math tomorrow?" she asked Edin.

He nodded but his eyes were drawn to Rigley, interested in what he had to say.

"Come on. Just tell me if you do or you don't."

"Okay, we can go home in a few. Or if you have enough

money for the bus. Better that than the embarrassing sedan that woman drives. People will think we're going to a funeral."

Edin pointed at Rigley, who was now acting like he was gasping for air.

"Yes! There is a specimen of stupidity next to me wasting his air talking when he should be studying to bring up our team GPA, which he so courteously brought down with last week's math test."

She turned to Rigley, exasperated.

"So then, what?"

Rigley swallowed it all down in a theatrical gulp.

"Nothing."

Several minutes of studying later, Zionée dropped her pencil and kept her eyes on the formula in the chemistry page. "No, I will not. And do not. Want to look at it."

"It's like a little mirror!" laughed Principal Flores. The office light was mixed in with a little bit of the blue remaining in the morning sky and the smell of the cafeteria coffee cakes were already accenting the campus air.

"I don't smile," Zionée said in monotone.

"Well, you should," Flores said as she closed the book and chuckled. "You can't let them get to you. Whether it is real or not – you just gotta keep a firm grasp on the present. So how are things? With the team?"

"Detrimental. Can I leave?"

"No."

"No, I mean – can I leave the Team Ranking System?"

"No, because I'd never forgive you."

"Oh I just thought it was because it was in your absolute authority as principal of this school to force me into doing this."

"I prefer the emotional blackmail."

Zionée stood up from her chair.

"How much more do I have to endure my classmates weaponizing this lie against me?" she shouted while tapping the yearbook. She had stolen it from Rigley after recalling the way he let himself get punched in the stomach to take it from Rickward.

"And what lie would that be?"

"Tessa Seredin. The idea that someone could be – no that

someone *is* better than me! To be worthy enough to be my mother! This is just a biological coincidence."

She clicked the tip of her tongue against her teeth to make an annoyed tisk before moving towards the door.

"Zionée," she said more sternly. "You're not doing this for me. And considering how I'm still trying to figure out how to explain to Malibu University why one of their school buses was found with an empty tank of gas, I don't think I owe you anything. Understand?"

Flores clicked her eyelids over her dark, brown eyes.

Zionée nodded slowly, bit her lower lip, and then clutched the hem of her skirt. She walked out the door without another word.

Yogun shakes the can of graffiti and sprays it at an incredible sight for Tessa to behold. They are in the underground basement of the school where only the janitors and higher up gang leaders are allowed to enter.

"It's called the Legendary Graffiti Mural."

"Legendary?"

Yogun shakes the can again and tosses it to Tessa.

"If you can keep it that way. Tell no one. The mural speaks for itself. Through everyone."

"I thought that's what the Internet was for," Tessa says, moving her gaze to take in all of the colors.

"It can be just as powerful."

Tessa squints her mind's eye, remembering all of the graffiti Yogun had Alonzo teach her how to read. The strange, multicolored labyrinth of letters sprawl from one end of the wall to the other with patterns of smaller, black font streaming across the middle like a riddle of thorns. Among the gangs of the public sector, they call it "graffligraphy", an art form that hides and distorts the alphabets of the English language in such a way that they are interconnected and interwoven with each other. Only trained eyes can decipher and take them apart to see the obscene, poetic secrets they keep.

"Ronnie J. is a –?"

Yogun laughs at the obscenity before she can finish saying it. Tessa is pointing on the section he had just sprayed over.

"I just sprayed over the word 'not'. Once the other leaders

come down, they'll circulate this rumor out into the whole campus."

"And then?"

"The higher ups of the other gangs will change the way they treat this kid. Once he starts getting respected, his friends will be too. Pretty soon, the friends of his friends will have to change the math of their targets. Speaking of which, you want to try?"

"What?"

He hands her the spraypaint.

"That thug with the stained shirt in class was really wounding you up, wasn't he?"

"I don't need your protection."

"Nah, I can tell since you make a point not to mention it. But this is your chance. He's a thug with not many friends in power, so he can't do anything about it. Anything he said about you, you can say about him. Spray whatever you like on the mural about the guy. He'll never mess with you again."

Tessa hesitated as she reached halfway for the spray can before deciding not to. She shakes her head.

"Thanks."

Yogun chuckles.

"Looks like you learning fast. The literacy of the streets."

In the next few weeks, the school's social hierarchy starts to reorganize itself around this rumor and to Tessa's amazement, small groups that were previously game to humiliation, start to switch roles with their abusing powers. They continue her curriculum with graffligraphy and with each lesson she gets more literate.

"When you said you were going to teach me the literacy of the streets," Tessa asks Yogun as they take their seats in class next to Alonzo.

"You thought I mean it literally?"

"Yeah."

Yogun watches Tessa unwrap her injured and slightly broken right hand and chuckles. Although she is now quickly considered Yogun's second-hand man, she is still not safe from her own temper. The blood staining the loose edge of her bandage wrap reminds her of one of the graffligraphy letters in the mural, rhyming with both the shape and color of the character.

"See that fool over there?" Alonzo says to her, pointing at a mean-faced kid sitting a few desks away, "Isn't that the guy who messed with you last week?"

"Yeah?"

"Don't you want to get revenge? I mean he messed this fool up real bad. Maybe even a friend."

"I don't have any friends."

"He was a private."

Tessa's eyes widen.

"What are you trying to say?"

"Nothing man," Alonzo says, a little disappointed. "Nothing."

They hear a loud thud. Tessa turns to the window. A body is thrown to the hard glass, staining it with blood. Tessa puts on some earphones but her music overwhelmed by the sudden tidal rise of jeers and calls. Everyone around her rushes to the window with excitement despite the teacher's protest. People cheer on as the very dream that their parents held them up to be is eviscerated day after day. For them to not do anything about it makes her angry on one level. But their actual cheering and encouragement takes her fury and indignation several stories higher.

"Hey gringo," she hears some bold, new kid sitting a few seats away call at her. "You want to know what your momma told me last night?"

Without turning around, her eyes glower at a hate bigger than all of them. Any respect she can muster for her self or the love for the person that these remarks doubled up against starts to wear and tear from all the cracks made about her family, sexuality, and race. Yogun sits back, playing a video game amusedly. She finishes unwrapping her hand and ignores a ball of paper thrown at her eye. The kid walks up to her. His shoulders are wide but she can tell that he is shorter. He spreads his arms out threateningly to intimate the question of "what". Tessa sighs, refusing to give in, knowing better how this gesture is built from years of nobody caring to ask. The bold, bald thug rubs her hat aggressively, messing up her hair a little and she almost considers grabbing his wrist and twisting it. The agility is always open to her. The power. But did it say anything important?

The creep continues his way to find some fresher, prey more prone to humoring him. Tessa, Yogun, and Alonzo remain quiet.

Sometimes, jerks like these come rushing to her after lunch and beg for forgiveness after they realize she isn't just sitting next to *the* Derrion Yogun. Others remain cruel and blissful in their ignorance.

Everybody in Yogun's gang is supposed to take care of one another. Under a small tree by the bungalows, the injured gather when they don't want to deal with the school nurse writing them up for fighting. It is Tessa's turn this week to tend to the wounds of the losing ones. She is helping bandage up a particularly nasty bruise on a kid named Marco. When she comes back from getting bandages to tend to the same bruise, it is now on a different arm. To her surprise it is the same kid who beat up Marco.

"What are you doing here?"

"Gang rules."

"Where in the rulebook says you got to mess with your own gang?"

The kid looks away.

"Look, you understand nothing. I heard rumors that he was talking bad about my dad behind my back."

Tessa looks at the bruise and feels her own sore arm mirror the unpleasant feeling.

"So you gave each other this on a rumor?"

He glares at her. She returns it with a tough squint.

"What do you care?"

"Because when people do this to each other it makes me sick. And I don't like being sick. Call it selfishness."

Some of the other gang members gather around, listening to the shadow of their leader becoming audible in front of them for the first time.

"So the only way I can stomach it is to learn the way pain travels through each and every one of our miserable, rotten lives. Where it goes and why. Reading from that bruise, you messed around with him, didn't you? Instead of straight up asking if he was talking about your dad, you used that feeling as an excuse to be a total punk. So you probably said stuff about his dad too."

Tessa looks to Marco, who is one of the students watching. Marco turns to face the thug. He is either too angry or too guilty to return his gaze at first but he eventually does. The familiar exchange in their eyes seems to agree with her suspicions.

"So you got off on punking him – afraid that you may go too far – maybe you did go too far. But hey he's fighting back now, so why shouldn't you? Show him his place. All the while holding on to that feeling in your heart – daddy's honor and not wanting to disappoint it – all until it comes down to this."

She presses the bruise until the kid screams in pain and punches her. The tree branch above them rattles from a brief gale and a few leaves fall. The others move in but she holds her hand out, shaking her head. She gets up off the ground and points at the newly forming purple on her cheek.

"And now you've told it to me as well."

There is no applause. No cheers. Everyone just looks at each other, dumbfound. Emilio, the kid with the deep, black bruise walks up to Marco and they show each other the temporary tattoos they gave one another. Marco's fingers on his free hand are too injured to finishing wrapping the bandaging without pain. Emilio takes the wrap and finishes bandaging for him. Though they still hate each other's guts, they can both see it more clearly now. The conditions around them and the corruption building within come from the same place.

4 – Accelerated Learning

Rigley was sound asleep when he heard the classroom door slam open. Period two was always the hardest class to stay awake through. In first period, Weavins was too strict of a teacher for anyone to get away with sleeping in his class. He bolted up, stirring with a shell-shocked panic.

"I'm up! I'm done studying!"

It was his pre-calculus teacher, Professor Xen, coming in with his suitcase, his preppy getup, his thin glasses, and earphones.

"Oh. Hey Xen."

"Oh hey?" Xen said with his eyebrows raised. "You know there are many great stereotypes to break and having no manners when you're Chinese doesn't strike me as a particularly bold choice."

"Neither does having an English accent," sneered Debby, who was sitting a few seats away. Zera laughed with an obligatory riff in her tone. Rigley stuck his tongue out in their direction and then watched with sleep-deprived eyes as Professor Xen started taking out small, square sheets of paper and folding them. Rigley's reflexes were sharpened to dodge or catch a crumpled paper ball. Although he had studied progressively this time, at the expense of DDR with his cousins, he was still nervous as he watched those fingers fold each paper with a selective sense of care. The level of quality in which he folded the origami reflected the student's grade. Rigley was often surrounded by crumpled paper cranes and wobbly-legged frogs. He had run out of ways to joke about how his crunched up test score was supposed to look like any animal.

"Think faster, Kurosawa!"

Suddenly a sharp paper-plane flew right above his eye. Edmondo and a few other classmates laughed but Rigley ignored them. To his awe, he unfolded it and found a shining B-. While still one of the lowest grades in the class it was a leap in progress. Laughing snidely, he began doodling a little Anime version of himself until Zionée sat down next to him, staring with admonishment with that cold, muscular scowl.

"What are you laughing about? We're still the lowest team on the scoreboard."

"Yeah?"

Rigley stopped and looked at her. He moved his mouth like he was chewing a piece of bubble gum, only he wasn't. They completed their conversation with a bitter smile humbling each other as they squinted slowly with mutual detestation. Then they turned away from one another and did not communicate for the rest of the class. Rigley crumpled the paper from his notepad and got up to sit somewhere else.

On his way around the class, he sniffed his nose from some dust and allergies. He noticed Cory pulling a chair out from underneath Hashim's desk, waiting for him to sit down. As soon as he turned away, back to some obscure conversation about a family holiday to the Catalina Isles, Rigley moved Hashim's chair back in place. However, as Zera happened to be seated right next to him that day, he decided to move it back out. Hashim returned from the bathroom and Rigley gestured that his seat was where Zera was sitting. When Zera returned from picking up a parent's note at the office, she did not notice that her stuff was moved to where Hashim had been sitting. Zera yelped, falling in an awkward manner over the space of her misplaced chair and everybody laughed. Rigley stopped laughing when he noticed that Cory and Debby were laughing too. He shook his head and went over to Edmondo's table, where he quietly annoyed his way in to their conversation on a TV show that they were mocking.

Back at her desk, Zionée secretly un-crumpled Rigley's paper and looked at the drawing.

Vicky's training had been paying off. One lunch afternoon, she showed up to school collecting them with great difficulty from across all of their different hangout spots. Zionée was lecturing to freshman in her economics club, Edin was in the library, and Rigley was eating lunch in Professor Behring's empty classroom in the history building. When Vicky found him, he had a string of gum from his mouth connected to the underside of desk table as he prepared to write a new insult.

They met up together at the courtyard. She was wearing an orange jump suit and gave the impression of having jogged over from a very far place.

"You... three... need to start hanging out together... more..." panted Vicky.

"Do you have asthma?" Zionée asked.

Vicky raised an eyebrow at her before wiping the sweat off of it and then shaking her head.

"No."

"Then it should be fine."

Edin stared quietly into space, not daydreaming but listening. At the same time, he could feel the flutter of the autumn breeze whistling a play of light leaves, gold and green, through the air. The concept of being on a team was still very strange to him.

Vicky glanced at him and blinked to get his attention.

"Hey there, leaves of grass?" she asked. "You listening?"

He turned his head to her and was about to nod.

"Yes," Zionée answered for him.

Vicky looked at her and continued to yawn. This time it sounded more like a sigh.

"And all three of you? Are you all right?"

"You know how they say you shouldn't ask if a person is all right if they're really not?"

"Huh, funny I don't," Vicky began, loudly talking over Zionée. "Anyways. We're at the bottom of the league."

"So what miracle have you got in mind?"

Vicky started oinking and making snorting sounds like a pig. Rigley laughed at this as Edin became awkward.

"You hear that?"

"What?"

"That's you hogging the airtime!"

Zionée made a frustrated noise. Vicky looked to Rigley and Edin.

"I'm sleepy. You have lunch yet?" Rigley asked. She laughed because his accent always amused her when he spoke.

"Meet me in the city park this weekend. And bring rope. And bicycles. And maybe a first-aid kit. Helmets too."

They arrived with all of the items on the list checked that Saturday. The grass was freshly laminated with the cold, morning dew. Vicky arrived late as usual and was halfway changed out of her blue swimsuit uniform. She put on the orange jump-suit jacket again.

"You're on a swim team, Vicky?" Rigley asked.

"Water tennis. Varsity!"

Rigley and Zionée exchanged looks of perplexity. Edin winced a little as Vicky dried her hair with a towel, causing small flecks of water to hit him.

"Did you all bring bikes?"

They nodded and pointed at their bikes parked along side the fences. She smiled in a way that caused the freckles in her face to stir. Their inevitable question as to what this was all about was answered in the ferocious momentum of the next few hours. Vicky forced them to bike with an elastic band of black rope tied to their frames and drove her van behind them at increasing speeds. This resulted in a lot of crashes and injuries, which complimented the presence of Edin's first-aid kit nicely.

They collapsed onto the grass to catch their breaths and left their bikes resting flat alongside them. Edin sat up and slapped the largest band-aid he could find on the huge scab on his knee.

"Doesn't that hurt?" Rigley asked.

"Yes," Edin partially mouthed. Suddenly they could hear the roar of the engine growing loud and close as Vicky caught up to them again. She stopped and got out of her van. Her face was calm and friendly but with an intense fire in her eyes amplified by the brightness of her orange jacket.

"Again!"

"We've been biking and running for hours!" Zionée complained.

"So? And what have you learned?"

"That you're a sadistic –"

Rigley clapped his hand over Zionée's mouth while Vicky smiled lazily in what he found to be a threatening way. The leaves continued to roll through the air around them. For what seemed like hours, the only sounds that they could hear were a few birds chirping, some fell branches rattling, and the furious metal clicking of bike gears as they pedaled. After another couple of rounds when they still couldn't come up with an answer, they marched achingly back to their bikes. As soon as they heard the engine starting up behind them they began pedaling. They were all covered in so many bandages and wrappings that by the end of the second weekend of this training they had lost track of how many times they had fallen. Finally, upon the third weekend, Rigley devised an answer. Vicky had tied the rope to their ankles this time and told them to run the entire bike loop. After one particularly unsynchronized jump that caused them to all fall and stumble, he called for her.

"Vicky!"

"Figured it out? About time!"

"What?"

Zionée glared to the side with a slight twirl of her eyes. Rigley looked from her to Edin. Vicky finished her ice cream and then she took out the first-aid kit.

"Rigley. You procrastinate and don't save enough energy until the very last minute. That's why you slow everyone down at turns and cause everyone to crash. Be more consistent."

Vicky slapped him in the arm where his injury was healing and he winced in a direction that caught him the sight of a hummingbird floating near his bike.

"Zionée, you bike too fast! It's really that simple. With these ropes, you can't easily pull the team up to your speed all on your own. You need to rely on your teammates and trust them to synchronize with you at their own pace."

Zionée didn't speak. Rigley realized she had tried to slow down at the sharp turns on the road the past weekend. Vicky tried to put a bandage on one of her injuries but she took it and applied it by herself instead.

"Edin, you have caused crashes consistently because of your

hesitation to communicate. If you're going to turn, you have to do whatever it takes to let them know."

After putting a bandage on the new scab on his knee, she sighed.

"Inspiring speeches of perseverance and hope and all don't mean anything until you start doing. Come on, I'll drive you all back to school."

When she dropped them off in front of Sheltevue, she walked with them to the grass ledge. She held her fist out.

"Where are we in this, you guys?"

Zionée looked coldly off to the side while Edin looked down at his shoe. Rigley placed his fist against her knuckles.

"Together," replied Rigley.

Slowly, Edin placed his hand on top of their hands until finally, Zionée did too. Vicky smiled and punched Rigley's knuckles where they were wounded. He winced and pulled back, gasping with a look of surprise.

"Remember that every time your hand gets tired from studying. Zionée? Edin?"

"We're good," said Zionée.

During the following weeks, they ate lunch and sat together in every class they shared and camped out in the city library, staying up into the darkest depths of the night. One afternoon, Rigley sat on top of the metal cafeteria table, placing his feet on the blue, metal weaving pattern of the seats. He stared through the holes, concentrating to detect what small moments of life were moving. Then he looked up at the multiple arrays of his classmates, all chattering about and meaning something to each other, going through things together. In his safety and sanctuary, observant and alone, he began to notice what Edin had too. All of the other teams had most of its members pre-organized to this effect, more or less. They weren't plotted against each other nor were they the targets of some grand scheme of sabotage.

Late at nights, they would shuffle the hours of deep sleep between studying and guarding one another. Vicky called this technique the Sleeper Guard Shuffle. After one particularly grueling session, Zionée was surprised with Rigley's insistence to be the last one to stay up. He grabbed her notes from her side of the table.

"Come on, I'll take the notes down for you for this class. You can trust me."

"You won't fall asleep?"

"I won't."

"I'm really tired but... I can handle it."

"Zionée."

"Rigley."

It was as quiet as deep space between them.

"All right."

"Thanks," she said burying her face in between the pages of the history book. "I'm just going to... highlight..."

Edin watched Vicky staring at them from her table surrounded by all of her heavy college textbooks. She walked over to him and nodded at his work. Then she looked at Rigley, who was struggling with the calculus problems.

"Not again, I thought we went over how to do this, Rigley," she said, yawning. He shook his head and rubbed his eyes. "Hey, pay attention to the exercise examples."

"I do, but they're not the same as the problem."

"Would you still feel like a genius if they were? Keep trying. I'll come back in a few."

"What are you working on?"

"O-chem."

She walked over to her table and sat back down; touching her homework sheets that she was having problems with herself. A girl with curly, blonde hair walked up to her and nodded up at her.

"Sup," Debby said. "You're Vicky, right?"

"Can't find your team?"

"No, we're parked outside because we went to go get food."

"Nice."

"I heard about you from my brother. You were pretty chill around here last year. Wished we hung out."

"Were you a freshman?"

"Yeah, but I mean, I didn't act like one."

Vicky nodded and looked back down at her paper.

"So you want to stop by our car and hang out? I hear that calculus problem is a real pain but we're way on top of it."

"Don't I wish my team was as well-balanced as yours?"

"Don't you?"

Vicky closed her chemistry textbook and folded her hands over it, recalling a moment earlier that afternoon when Zionée was frustrated with Rigley because of the same math problem.

"Sure, they can get on my nerves," Vicky sighed. "And it does make it a lot harder to guide them through their different skill sets. I'm sure if I were your Team Counselor, it might be easier. Not a lot of things worse than a teacher abandoning her students."

"Zionée could name a few, I'm sure."

Debby curled her lips at this.

"Oh yes, and then there is that. Whatever business it is of yours though, I can't fathom. You've got to be pretty insecure to have to look for something bad about someone and make it everyone's business rather than focusing on your own."

"All right, fine, Vicky-sensei," Debby sneered. "I get it. You won't help us."

"I'm not your sensei. I am Team Omega's. And I trust they'll pull through, however frustrating it is to watch. At Sheltevue, none of your teachers will ever turn your back on you. Notice that? It isn't because you're smart, Debby. It's because it's part of the lesson. And seeing as I'm still waiting for you to return my note sheet I was working on to show Rigley how to correct his math problem, I'm not too certain if you got it yet."

Debby pulled out a piece of paper and slammed it on the table, blushing with shame and admonishment.

"Don't tell my TC," she muttered.

Vicky walked back to Rigley's table where he was still scratching his head as he idly doodled around then numbers. She placed the paper down. Edin looked up at her.

"I didn't see Debby sneak it off the table," Rigley said sleepily. "My bad."

"It's cool, buddy," Vicky laughed. "You see what I did here?"

She pointed at the problem where it had shown directions on how to integrate the problem to get the answer. Debby had excitedly circled it with her pen.

"Do the opposite of that."

"Take the derivative?"

"Hey, she got you stranded on a beach."

Rigley looked down for a moment and then at Edin, who was taking small sips of lemonade juice.

"No, she got them stranded with me."

"Then it's our luck to deal with now," Vicky said simply. She walked back to her table as he and Edin exchanged looks and nodded, getting back to work as the hour dial spun.

When they arrived at the local arboretum for their next training session, they got on their bikes at the top of the hillside and stared out into the horizon. The low, blanket of mist was slowly dispersing in the bright, crepuscular sunrise. The wet, grassy scent rode the cold air to their noses as they watched the small, familiar white van, like a pit-bull with wheels, careening around the slopes of the nearby hills. Vicky parked at the top of the hill and then walked out to the back of her truck to get something. Then she turned around and stared at their sleepy faces. It was the only time of day that her face didn't appear sleep-deprived and the natural darkness under her eyes was invisible under her morning makeup. Rigley yawned as Vicky turned away to get the bike chains, sparing them of any conversation and to get right to it. Rigley rubbed his tired eyes and turned to Zionée.

"I took a video class at school once."

She turned her squinted eyes at him and nodded without smiling.

"Do you know what a dolly zoom is?"

She shook her head as Edin yawned once before drying the handles of his bike from condensation.

"I think my eyes can dolly zoom. Because the horizon around Vicky's car appears to be moving."

Zionée turned and her eyes sprung awake with panic.

"Vicky!"

Vicky turned around and walked over to the entrance to the back of the van, not noticing at first that it felt like walking on a slow treadmill.

"Yeah?"

Edin and Zionée both gaped at her as the car started to tilt away under the growing tug of gravity. Rigley looked at them.

"So your eyes can dolly zoom too?"

"Vicky!"

"What?"

The car jerked forward and she almost fell back. Then she grabbed on to the side handle, watching them as they shrunk in the distance. Zionée kicked Rigley's foot, causing it to move his bike stand up, and getting him to start biking with them immediately. Together, they all accelerated as fast as they could down the slope after Vicky. Her van was approaching a small crater on the concrete. As they got closer, they skidded to a halt, drifting slightly their wheels to the side and finally came together in synchronicity. Although the distance was far from closed, Vicky threw the chain at them and they each grabbed hold of an end of it. They began a rapid game of tug of war with gravity, which they knew they could only win if they beat it in the race to Vicky. As soon as the van got far enough for the chain to extend to its full length, she grabbed on to the other end and jumped forward, rolling onto the street as her car hit the bump and flipped over sideways. Zionée, Rigley, and Edin biked over to her and got off their cycles to help her up. She winced from her scabs and injuries, now making her seem an awful lot like one of them.

"Parking brake," she said.

They took out the medical kit and started helping her bandage up. After Vicky called her insurance, her bad mood dissipated and she took them out for burgers. At the table near the window, Vicky watched the toll truck pull her car off and she waved out with a grateful smile. They anxiously overheard on the phone that the damage was covered but that the repairs were going to take about a month. Vicky took a sip of her soda and watched all three of them impulsively chewing their burgers at the same time. She took out her wallet and sighed with an airy smile.

"So, our next team mission is… putting our money together for the bus."

After another all-nighter in the library, Zionée woke up from the tickle of heat caressing her sleepy face coming from a warm cup of coffee placed next to her, their combined notes were completed on the table but Rigley was gone. Edin received a text message from Vicky and then showed the message to his sister. It asked if the technique was successful or not. Zionée looked around for Rigley, only to finally tap his foot with her own. He was collapsed on the floor, asleep.

"Reply yes," Zionée told Edin.

During math, when Rigley came back to his table, the mirage of seeing Zionée sneaking a peak at his Anime drawing dissolved quickly. She had un-crumpled it and began refolding it into a paper crane. Silently, without a word, Zionée handed the origami to him and then gave him a half-smile, free of any sarcasm, before opening her book to the next chapter on differential equations.

Tessa, now impressively literate with her graffligraphy, goes to the mural increasingly on her own now. Yogun steps into the school basement one afternoon and sees how much it is changed. When he reads the world-threatening new matrix of gossip, he momentarily loses his usually calm, high. Several areas of graffligraphy are obscured. Some spots are completely rewritten with new spray-paint. Stumbling, he recollects a little balance and turns to her.

"Tes, man, are you insane?" he shouts. "What have you done?"

She tosses the spray-can back to him.

"Isn't it funny how the power to change the world is in one small can of graffiti?"

Yogun runs his hand through his dreadlocks and shakes his head.

"You're crazy, you know that?"

Tessa scoffs and points at the dark, blue smears winding in and out of the black letterings.

"Every day, the powerful and the popular pick on the ones who are too weak to stand up for themselves. Whether it's selling drugs, local snobbery, or bullying, it is happening. Now it's time for something different to happen. Trust me, I'm on to something."

Yogun sighs, disconcerted by this.

"I won't argue with you. But just be ready when they do."

"I will be," she says after pausing contemplatively and staring up at the mural.

5 – Team Omega's Secret Weapon

As another week begins, Tessa moves through the private sector hallways alone. As she turns around the corner at the stairway, the privates rudely run past her and up the stairs, hopping up two steps at a time. From under her hat, she stares at them strangely as she slightly tilts her neck to crack it. She starts moving up the steps on the opposite side of the rail one by one when a public shoves past her, pursuing a smaller, spectacle-wearing kid. He pushes the kid against the rail, almost making him flip over to the other side. When they start kidding around and using racial slangs, Tessa stops and listens to echoes of their conversation spiral above her as they disappear up the next flight. Recent and unhealed emotional wounds of this still unfamiliar anachronism continue to sting from hearing it. She doesn't remember having to care about her race, sexuality, or family until people started insulting it so much. Then some privates, a Russian boy and a wavy-blonde girl with large, owl eyes walk past her snickering. A beautiful African-American T.A catches up to them and laughs with them.

"Some people can be so ghetto," the Russian boy says.

"They probably weren't taught right," adds the T.A. "Language that eloquent."

"That kid should tell on somebody," the wavy blonde girl says. "It's disgusting how he was treated and they're still friends."

"At least they have it easier in class," the T.A says. "And still some of them find a way to get distracted and make it like it's the hardest thing in the world."

Tessa starts to glare at them until the T.A turns and notices her.

"Young man, you need help finding the dean's office?"

She gasps slightly and shakes her head.

"Then you should probably get to class."

Tessa watches all three of them stare at her inquisitively before becoming annoyed by how they must be gluing her to the large, permanent marker graffiti on the wall behind her with their eyes. She turns around and goes back down the stairs. It is a while before she hears their feet shuffle on again and she suspects they lingered to watch her with that condescending reservoir of distrust.

Later at lunch, Tessa sits in the cafeteria table, eating some fries at an idle pace while Yogun talks to an Asian exchange girl in the angled shade of the umbrella. Sitting a few tables away, Alonzo and Marco lightly punk around with Emilio by the cafeteria table. After sharing the same type of hand bandages for a couple of weeks, they seem to be healing together as friends. She notices Yogun and the private, Samantha, stare at her for a brief moment as they talk.

"That's him, huh? The one my friends have been talking about."

"Hey, he's cool. Just because you've been in a fight doesn't make you a bad person."

"They say he does a lot more than just get into fights."

"Nah, he's cool. He's approachable."

Alonzo sits down and pours more ketchup on her fries. He then pretends to flinch in front of Samantha's friends standing nearby. Tessa scoffs while looking down, not caring to eat it anymore.

"The great Tessa Seredin. Man, they're talking about you like you're some kind of new devil fire. Not just the publics now."

"Guess I'd better not disappoint," Tessa says confidently.

Tessa's training in the literacy of the streets continues as she starts to kick in enough effort in school to keep her grades improving from the bottom of a dangerously low average. She squirts a water gun that she found in a broken-up locker up at the hallway mirrors. The small, sharp threads of water connect with the dusty panels of glass running above the lockers, rinsing it clear. Yogun holds his book up to his head as they arrive at the stairway.

"It's cool that you always start off wanting to defend someone," says Yogun, in a critical tone. "Yo, I respect that. But when you get into it, I can almost smell the green spent from all those karate lessons."

"It's not karate. If I'm not careful with it, I could end up in juvenile court."

Yogun puts on his reading spectacles.

"Whatever, down here that comes off as posh. If you're only doing it because you want to prove that you're better, who does that put you in the same league with?"

Tessa stops walking and notices a couple of bullies nearby slapping the back of a smaller kid's head at the bottom of the stairs.

"No, I'm not in their league."

Yogun shakes his head impatiently. But he doesn't raise his voice.

"Then tell me if it's ever been about winning a fight. You wanted to learn, so why you ditching half the lesson? You need to get sophisticated, Tessa. Fast. It's not just the injuries that spell out something. It's every punch or blind jab thrown."

"Out of what?"

"Guess you do know what kind of questions to ask."

At lunch, she hears more slurs in the background conversations, becoming numb to the impact of it, and realizes that where pride makes its home in is also where the desperate and the angry came to try to take it most. Race, sexuality, economic status, and family are about the only capital they seem to have a handle of to feel rich and also to make others feel poor. Tessa can feel the stubbornness of her own bits of bigotry start to loosen from her heart like barnacles off of a whale. She begins using less profanity after becoming self-conscious that this habit simply comes from the implicit association she makes with publics. Perhaps with enough power, she is not so different from the privates. Yogun pats her arm and points at a couple of thugs beginning to throw down in the nearby table.

"If you can read the rhythm of their rage, then you can follow it back to your heart," Yogun says. "You can learn what fuels this world; what ignites the hate in it."

As Tessa looks closer, they are actually standing up for a friend who is having his head smeared to the cafeteria table while the others pour milk on him. The police guards are never in sight until the fight itself breaks out. Sometimes they don't show up.

"Otherwise you're just a bully and it doesn't take a lot of brains to do that."

Tessa finishes unwrapping her newly healed knuckles and hands the bandaging to him. She walks over to where a ninth grader is being slapped around by his friend and laughing. As fast as a jolt of lightning, she throws the first punch and the punks answer with a storm of hooks. This time, her fists reciprocate momentum with the same blind fury. By the time the cops come and pull them apart, Tessa is on the ground, choking on blood and moving all of her bones painfully to make sure that none of them are broken. The school security cops, both used to having to take Tessa in, stare and laugh at her. Some of the students around them exchange uneasy looks. She closes her eyes for a moment, hearing only the static growl of the police officer's walkie-talkie picking up alien sounds distilled to a noise that is all but inaudible. Marco goes and helps her back up on her feet.

As she rises, she notices the other members of the crew nodding with respect. She slowly begins to see the strength of their community. There is loyalty that makes them valuable to one another.

On the giant digital scoreboard in the middle of the main hall, the numbers clicked and beeped. Zionée watched as their team ranking changed positions with another team in the middle.

In the corner of the school's botanic quad, the afternoon light arranged itself around the green patches not covered by the shadow of the trees. Edin popped a soda lid and began drinking while his sister sat down beside him quietly with an unfamiliar expression on her face. It was a smile. Zionée noticed the way Edin looked at her. Upon becoming aware of her sudden trespass, she took the soda from his hand and drank from it until she had an excuse to wipe it off of her mouth. Edin looked down on his hands. They sat in front of the aged, gray school statue, which had obscured features due to incomplete funding that was supposed to be going to its restoration. It stood, armored in a time capsule of ink formed out of the little bits of tagging covering all over its stone flesh. They could have been letters of disappointment for all of the broken promises the statue stood for or merely insignificant incidences of vandalism. Edin searched the smooth and un-sculpted face for where the nose and the lips might have protruded. He didn't touch his lips or his nose. Instead he looked back at his sister for a moment before shaking his head with gentle denial at his own wishful thinking.

"Did you finish your lunch?" Zionée asked.

Edin took his bento box out and revealed his uneaten rice and sandwich. On days when he couldn't hang out with Zionée or Rigley because the both of them were busy, he wouldn't eat his lunch. Rigley often talked of throwing his backpack off the second floor balcony of their history building and reminded him to be grateful that his food didn't reek through its container like his did.

"We got to think of some way to get you to not be afraid of where you eat," said Zionée.

He shuffled his afterschool lunch box away quietly and neatly as she stood up.

"Okay. Let's go home."

They went to the bus station and waited with the comforting certainty of being on time. Each adoption was like taking a bus to a new stop with a different social class. As Zionée worked harder and harder at school and community service, it turned into a job application process. Their resume contained memories of so many different foster homes, the first of which were the lower class stops. After getting off the bus, they arrived home in a small cult de sac of blue and white suburban houses. This time the stop was upper middle class. Zionée walked through the wide, open front lawn and into the two-story house. Effortlessly ignoring their most current roster of fosters, who inquired about why they had to take the bus, they made their way to their still unadjusted rooms. All that was laid out in their rooms was a minimalist set of boxes and a set of customized Japanese style uniforms in their closets. In the center of her bedroom was a single, economically designed desk with a CD-player lamp. They were always prepared to leave and never fully unpacked.

On some nights, when they didn't have to go home, Zionée and Edin volunteered community service hours with the school janitors. As a bonus she was given the keys to the science lab. One night, after calling home to make sure Edin had arrived safely back on his own, she stayed in by herself. Inside the cabinets was an impressive set of chemical substances. She had collected it for years from the unused leftovers of various experiments and stowed it away secretly so that no one, not even Professor Weavins, could use them for any assigned labs.

Zionée switched on a single lamp, turning her workspace into a lonely island of light in middle of the dark room. Her schoolbooks were neatly stacked and ready to be devoured. She quickly opened the shiny, new hardcover AP Chemistry textbook to the page of a multiple step problem. Weavins would sometimes have them do these marathon problems in groups as a class. She rarely participated because watching Rigley struggle made her almost as sick as having to share the eventual achievement with the group. As she struggled with the complexity of the problem, the sky grew dark. The clicking hand of the clock haunted her heartbeats, which were urgent beneath her breasts. The chemicals were bubbling around her effervescently, hot and dangerous. She resisted the urge to smash something while her concentration slipped with the accuracy of her recalculated boiling point.

The sound of the door opening after the fourth dizzy turn around her chair caused her to stir. As her rotating seat slowed to a halt she started to see the dark, black hair and curious brown eyes.

"You're early," said Rigley, gently yawning. He was not awake enough to be vividly surprised by all of the chemicals scattered about. "Science fair?"

"No – no this is just… oh. Shoot!"

Her CD-player alarm showed that it was twenty minutes till school started and she quickly slammed the snooze button before the music could start.

"Lock the door!"

"What?"

"Just do it!"

Rigley obliged and locked it from the inside. Zionée, remembering the backdoor, went to lock that one too. She ran to her chemicals and began pouring them all down into the sink. Rigley quietly joined her, closing his mouth so as not to inhale any lingering fumes. As he reached for a vat of red she quickly grabbed his wrist.

"No! Not that one!"

It was the closest configuration of a possibly accurate solution to the equation she could find. She had to keep it as a liquid milestone, if anything. Carefully she poured it in her last glass test-tube and bottled it shut. Then she and Rigley packed up all of her unused chemicals in their boxes and put them back in her special cabinet. The lock turned and clicked. Zionée stowed the key neatly away in her left pocket. After Rigley turned around for a brief moment, she quickly changed it to the other pocket. They unlocked the door just as the school bell rang.

As their classmates shuffled in with their daily complaints about homework, the cold morning air began to mix with the medical fumes of the usual chemistry supplies. They both took their seats by the sink tables near the windows. Rigley heard the small sound of a plastic lid pop off and turned to Zionée. She gave him a stick of Pocky and then attempted to suppress a cough but failed and the sound came out of her nose awkwardly. A stir of laughter came from behind them. Rigley glared back in the direction of the laughter. Zionée stared at him the whole time that he did.

"What?" said Cory. Rigley didn't say anything but continued to hold his gaze with intensity.

As they both finished their Pocky, they watched Hashim approach Zera at her seat while Edmondo did a last-minute review of the answers he got on the worksheet.

"Hi Zera," he began. "Did you do the titration problem on the homework?"

"So anyways, we're going to Catalina this weekend," said Debby. "You coming?"

"Yeah, I'd love to!"

"Don't fall off the boat this time," Rickward joked.

"Hey, shut up."

Rigley started playing with the sink faucet by moving the handles, opening and closing the water. Zionée closed it each time he opened it.

"Stop that!"

"Don't make me move you two," said Weavins, walking in with his book bag.

Rigley turned the faucet on again and this time Zionée slapped some of the water at his face before closing it.

"Never mind, I like this seating arrangement," Weavins quipped. The class laughed with sleep-deprived energy.

As Rigley wiped his face, he could hear Debby talking in the background.

"She can be such a…"

"Anybody watch the morning forecast today?" asked Weavins. "I came to school with an umbrella and everybody called me Asian because it got really bright. Rubbish weatherman."

Weavins turned on the projector and placed a plastic screen on it, beginning to write down some equations.

"All right, since my wife has a sweet tooth, I'm going to show you the chemical abbreviations for chocolate."

Rigley turned around again having heard Rickward and Debby snickering obnoxiously. Hashim rubbed his eyes while Edmondo feverishly scribbled in corrections for a homework problem last minute.

"Edmondo, you'd better not be doing what I think you're doing."

"If what you're thinking is that I'm checking my work with Hashim's answers, then yes."

"Yeah, no. I think you're checking your incomplete work with his answers."

"It's just a couple of problems, Weavins."

"Right, no excuse. Give me that. Everyone turn in your homework."

"Nice one," Rickward muttered as Edmondo complained under his breath while reluctantly handing in his homework first.

Weavins started walking around the science room, collecting their stoichiometry sheets. Rigley sighed, taking his out and tossing it down on his desk without any of the pride Letitia did so with in the seat next to him. Zionée bit her lip as she looked over her answers but couldn't help turning around at Debby every now and then, her face growing red. Finally Weavins went up to Rigley and watched him as he started scribbling.

"Oh, this one has to do it right in front of me, huh?"

"No, just adding something," he said.

There was laughter coming from the table behind them from the building chatter between the snobs. Weavins took a closer look at his paper.

"Why are you balancing Zinc with Chocolate?"

"It's not Zinc. It's Zionée. If I prove with this formula that she can digest chocolate then there's no way she's a bitch."

Weavins arched his eyebrows up in confusion before taking his homework assignment. Rigley turned around at Debby, who was now frowning for a moment before smiling innocently.

"Got that, Debby?"

Zionée stopped biting her lip and looked at him. After class, she waited for him for to walk to their next class together.

"You're waiting for me?"

"AP English is," she said. "Let's go."

As they walked down the stairs of the science building, she turned around to whisper to him between flights.

"You'd better keep what you saw today a secret."

"If you can trust me to."

Zionée blinked, speechless. Rigley's eyes moved down a little and then back at her.

"Right pocket."

Her smile faded and she looked at him challengingly.

"All right. After school."

They arrived back at the lab room at half past five. Edin was playing with an antique top, which he spun by pulling a string. It whistled majestically with a loud, wooden growl.

"Hey Edin."

Edin nudged his head up at Rigley in greeting and picked up the toy top, rewinding the string around it. Zionée pulled out a chair and pushed it towards him.

"Are we going to play a game?"

Zionée and Edin exchanged looks. All of the blinds were closed and the only lighting came from a few lamps.

"I feel like I'm about to be interrogated," joked Rigley.

"Sit here," said Zionée, gesturing to the chair.

Rigley cautiously obeyed and sat down. Edin finished winding the string around the top and set it to the ground again. As soon as he spun it, Zionée spun Rigley round and round. Only when he heard the sound of the noisy, wooden rattle fade away did the dark room stop spinning and he could hear Edin retrieving the top.

"If this is to prove I ate your last sushi during lunch, there are easier ways to ask."

Zionée looked at Rigley with her cold, green eyes. Getting uneasy, he blinked. Edin watched while idly rewinding the string around the top.

"How does it feel?"

"What?"

"Having the world revolve around you?"

"I don't understand."

"Don't worry, I'm going to help you to."

Her sentence completed with the sound of a sticky strap. Zionée had Rigley's wrists bound to the chair now.

"Wait, what are you...?'

"Edin?"

Edin whipped the top off of the string and it spun again and so did Rigley. The walls of the classroom, the chalkboard, and the faces of his friends melted with the momentum. The top fell to the ground, rolling loudly back into silence. By then, he thought he saw two Zionées.

"Look at me."

Rigley blinked and the two Zionées became one again.

"Egocentripetal motion."

"What?"

"Feelings."

"Okay?"

Rigley was relieved to hear the sound of the straps tearing off. He was now free to get up from the chair. His gaze followed Zionée as she walked across the lab to the secret spot in the cabinet, took out her key, opened it, and began unpacking the chemicals again.

"Is this what you're trying to do? Create a cure?"

Edin looked at him with his bemused, gray-blue eyes, sparkling green in the dark. Zionée set up the titration equipment, twisting nozzles meticulously and starting up flames to set the flasks on. Then she spread her formula sheets across another table.

"You're welcome, Rigley. Everybody's stuck in clockwise rotation. Every day, what do they all see? All of their problems in perfect centripetal orbit. I freed you. At least, momentarily. You'll find your method, I suppose. Mine is spinning counterclockwise against the direction of the world to remind me that I'm not in the center. But I'm not trying," she stopped to drop some copper in a boiling beaker, "...to be. And I'm not creating a cure. *This* is the cure. Doing this formula allows me to accomplish something that no one else can. And that knowledge to me alone is antidote enough."

"For what?"

"The things that keeps us from being useful while we're alive."

Zionée set the timer and waited as the colorful solutions and chemicals brewed next to her effervescently. Then she picked up the top and rewound the string around it. Rigley walked towards the chemistry book that was resting flat on its spine and saw the immense formula sprawled across two pages. Edin came and looked too.

"And what about the feeling of pride? Can you get rid of that too?"

Zionée stopped playing with the top for a moment. Edin looked from her to him.

"What?"

"Won't you feel that once you solve this problem?"

"No. That's the point."

Rigley looked at her, as the sound of the top hitting the floor in a violent, rapid waltz started again. Edin opened his mouth to speak but hesitated, feeling the air plucked from his lungs before he could draw them. Rigley looked at him and waited for him to speak.

"So this is your retort?" he said, turning back to Zionée. "Both of you?"

Edin looked back at his sister and then down at the top, having rolled next to his shoe.

"My what?"

"This is your answer to being food poisoned and left stranded on that beach?"

Edin picked up the top, his hands beginning to idly rewind and unwind it repetitively. He looked at his sister. Zionée walked towards Rigley. They were almost the same height.

"What are you trying to say?" she asked him threateningly.

"You spun around in a chair doing science problems instead of – "

"Instead of what? Get angry? You mean like you did?"

Rigley's eyes twitched a little. He didn't look away. Everything about him reflected in her piercing, green eyes rang true.

"We both know who did it. Everyone does. Our teachers. Our principal. And they got their detentions and suspensions. But you? You messed up our team GPA for the first four weeks because you were so busy being productive with your anger and your passion making stupid little Anime sketches. I've given you your chance. And you threatened to deliver us into incompetence and failure. Well, maybe you've built up the immunity to that sort of thing, but to people like my brother and me where we don't allow for that sort of thing to happen."

"Is this about the scholarship? You want to win it that –"

"It's about Darwinism. And I'm stuck struggling to survive," she uttered with hateful intensity, "with you."

He blinked and opened his mouth but didn't speak for a moment.

"How do you know about my sketches?" Rigley asked. Edin looked down at his shoes, avoiding his gaze. Zionée didn't answer him.

"Of course," Rigley said, looking knowledgeably at her as he remembered the Pocky.

"Coincidence of tastes doesn't make us soulmates."

"I wouldn't count on it."

As he started to turn and grab his things, Zionée raised her voice at him.

"Good, because you know what I think? You really are their secret weapon!"

Her words sank slowly in him like fresh, cutting knives. All of their hard work with Vicky, all those nights counting on each other, all of it felt undone in one sentence. Edin went to the chair and began spinning himself in counter clockwise. In his haste, he had forgotten to spin the top so he stopped to do that first before getting back on the chair. Rigley and Zionée looked at each other for what seemed like an eternity of scorn compressed into a minute.

As he moved through it, he was too angry to care or see where he was going. It was too dark to tell if he was walking through the public sector or the private sector. All he'd need to do was to turn on the keychain light on his backpack and if he saw a twin firefly, he'd know where he was. But he didn't. He thought about what would happen if he did try to fulfill his role in their enemies' design. Despite the devastation it would cause his self-esteem, he thought about the effect it would have on Zionée's. But it would also hurt Edin, who he did not blame. She must have put him through that ritual as well. He remembered clearly why Debby was insulting her this morning in class. The rumor was too awful to believe. But he now had the spite to. It must have been why Edin doesn't speak.

He continued walking, his breath growing shallow as he hastened almost into a jogging stride. She was correct to assume that he was going to relay most of that bitterness into producing more drawings, which he had been paranoid about doing in school ever since they had been going missing. What he could hardly believe was how, on that same morning, he thought that they were destined to become better friends by the end of the day. Perhaps they would have too, if he agreed to give up his egocentripetal-whatever it was, but it wouldn't have been the kind of friendship he'd want. Asking him to cheat was one thing but asking him to purge his feelings put everything he stood to lose into focus. He could see the snobs sitting at the grass at lunch, beautiful and cool, as they always were, like static impressions of routine, scenic and ornate. How in control of their feelings and how lazily casual they must be to judge others for things like snorting water through their nose or not having as culturally disciplined of a set of behavior. And yet, possessed as he was by this adrenaline, livened though he was by this anger, he looked around the dark corridor and found no company but shadows.

Vicky sat alone at the park that weekend on a bright, windy day. She received a text from Edin, which mentioned that they were all sick.

"With what?" she wondered.

Zionée stared at the back of the statue from the window of her class during period three. Something in her was starting to sculpt it into a shape.

"No, Rigley... that was a good attempt. But sit down and let somebody else try," said Professor Xen's voice.

"You suck, Rigley!" said Edmondo. Rickward, Debby, and Cory laughed.

"Hey, why don't you read between the lines?" Rigley said. He pointed to the way the line graph had two vertical lines on both the negative and positive ends of the horizontal x-axis.

"That doesn't make sense," said Hashim.

Zionée looked up at the board. At first she was expecting it to be completely wrong but upon closer inspection of the problem, Rigley had demonstrated a critical understanding of the cosecant graph and had almost gotten it right.

"Hey, who wants points deducted for being an asshole?" Professor Xen asked.

Several students in class gasped with surprise. It was unusual of him to be defending the usually bombastic class clown that always got on his nerves. He cleared his throat and started his lecture again on the next chapter.

Zionée looked down at her graphing paper. And then she took another peek at the Anime drawings she had stolen from him. As Xen walked over her desk in the midst of his sermon-like lecturing, she covered them with the graphing paper to look like she was double-checking her work.

The lunch bell rang and Rigley's attitude was attracting a large amount of drama and sycophantic bullying from his classmates. Their degrees of friendliness often fluctuated tumultuously throughout the year. Everyone's feelings seemed to be in orbit with something that made them so inconsistent on a day-to-day basis. Come exam time, the stress usually brought out the worst in a lot of them. But when it was over, a precipitation of amnesia suddenly occurred and instantly all was forgiven. Days approaching weekends or holidays insulated more friendliness. Days of hard, excessive class work encouraged them to fight harder to stay out of being bored. But every so often, there was a rare moment of darkness in one person's life that activated the evil of the group and attracted them like flies to something raw and hurting. A living wound in the soul visible through an increase in clumsy behavior and bitterness, something that they could poke and pry at, curious for what entertaining extroversions of emotions they could provoke to distract from the mundane.

Rigley spat on the ground as he walked his way through the halls and out into the hot, ethereal light of the open school grounds. The bubble gum was disorganized and messy under everyone's tables and he got so sick of it that he flipped one of the desks over while no one was around. In period one, Edmondo lent him a pencil but then in P.E was talking trash about how badly he played basketball in front of his soccer teammates. Cory talked him out of using his slingshot on Professor Nairs after she sarcastically ridiculed him. As soon as class was over, he pushed him into a large, big-boned classmate Hikari after class. When Cory saw Zera wince, he instantly apologized and said that he was only kidding. Although he sometimes saved a seat for Rigley in art class because he had no other private to sit with, Rickward slapped him upside the head once in front of Debby to get a laugh. In AP Spanish class, he suspected Hashim was going to stand up for him until Edmondo joined in on bashing his bad listening skills with Professor Esperanza. And Debby, who always said good morning to him in period one when nobody was around, would trash talk him nonstop when in class. The alchemy of their company stirred so many different sides in each of them that it made Rigley sick to try to keep up. He almost started to wonder if the only reason he wasn't like that was because he didn't have enough friends with to meet himself again in their different expectations. Everyone else met themselves over and over with a different face and tune to sing each time. This was the natural order of real life. No dramatic acts of coming to the rescue. If it ever occurred, it happened between friends whom were someone else's bullies or bullies whom were someone else's friends.

As he made his way down the hall, passing the trophy cabinet, he ran into Principal Flores. She smiled at him before bumping awkwardly into the assistant vice principal, who seldom showed up. The square jawed, perky woman laughed and continued her way while Flores picked her things up from the ground. Rigley overheard Professor Tammy make a snide remark at this by the doorway and was suddenly frozen in place.

"Rigley?" Tammy said, spotting him as she finished up her coffee cake. "Oh, hey Weavins, you have him for chemistry right? He's awesome."

"Isn't he just?" Weavins said slowly and sarcastically. Rigley found himself wishing it had been Weavins who made the snide remark. Anyone but his favorite teacher.

"Rigley, what's up?" asked Tammy, concerned. "You okay?"

He tried to smile at her but for some reason his muscles were pulling the corners of his mouth flat. Then he continued his way without saying anything.

"All right, see you in class," she smiled. He moved out the main building side exit, frantically building his pace across the hot, bright pavement.

Zionée walked into the history classroom and saw that no one was there.

"He's not here," she said over the phone.

"Well, that's where I found him last time," said Vicky.

"I know Edin says he comes here all the time. Hi Behring."

The portly, pale blonde-haired Professor Behring walked by and waved politely at her. His mouth was full with a sandwich, obscuring the sound of his greeting a little but Zionée caught that he meant to tell her to make sure to lock his classroom when lunch was over. But she did so as soon as he left. She noticed a desk was turned over and had lots of bubble gum underneath it.

As she looked it over, she was shocked to find that it said "bitch" consistently all throughout the calendar day slots, labeled with dried red and purple gum. She stopped on the most recent day and read it quietly aloud.

"Not bitch. Eats chocolate."

Zionée turned her seat back over and sat down on it. She laughed in spite of herself and turned to the locked door, seeing a few shapes pass by. Quickly checking the time, she took out Rigley's Anime drawings and some tracing paper. Anime consumed her negative free time with actual hobbies, which got her adrenaline going faster than a soccer goal or an A+ in math. She indulged in Manga, character CDs, online Anime, and building model kits of robot mechas. Constantly aware of how taboo the subject was amongst her classmates, she would never have brought it up until she saw Rigley's drawing. As he was Asian, she considered him to be more culturally licensed to exhibit this affinity. She had been sketching and tracing over Rigley's Anime characters for weeks now, trying her hardest to dig up the emotion it must have took to carve those lines that were building up the images that she thought were so interesting. Although this threatened to undo her own attempts to cure herself of all egocentripetal motion, she found it hard to stop her hand from riding the arc of the penciled eyes looking up at her. She was so afraid of those eyes but intrigued all the same. There was a knock on the door. Zionée scurried quickly to hide the drawings. She could see who it was from looking at the boyish silhouette and then took out her phone, which vibrated urgently.

Rigley was sitting quietly by the edge of the mound. He was like a fuse that was deliberately putting itself close to the fire. Most of them there looked like the kind of main characters the movies would have everyone rooting for because they were so hip and quirky in their own way. Their popularity was compulsory, having inherited their social circles from the same middle school. They were smart, funny, and athletic and had all-around personalities. They were the snobs. It was their emotions that elected all others and their attitudes that cooled all others. Debby, Rickward, Cory, and Zera walked past him. Cory deliberately tripped over his backpack so as to spill not only the contents of his lunch but some of his Anime art as well. His neck grew hot and red as they laughed and apologized before continuing their way to the large tree at the middle. He quickly became self-conscious about how bad his lunch smelled in a grassy hill full of brown bags containing normal, scentless sandwiches. Unable to stomach it anymore, he got up to leave.

"Hey Rigley!"

Ignore them. They called and called with the most sincere tone in their voices. He turned and faced them, every insecure muscle twitching painfully inside of him from the contrast they brought against him.

"Hey Rigley! Come hang out with us!"

Rigley impulsively readied his middle finger in one pocket of his blue sports jacket as he stood up and turned around. There was a gathering crowd of classmates, many of them watching from the volleyball and basketball courts. Others joined in by the fences to witness the tension that was collecting into the middle of the grassy mound.

"Unless you're too good for us that is," Rickward continued with a goofy scoff.

"Quite the opposite, really."

"So modest," Debby chuckled. "I love your accent."

"Do you?" Rigley smiled, reciprocating sarcasm.

"Yeah, come on bro. Why not?" Cory asked while shaking his sandy hair and throwing a few sweet looks at some nearby girls. Rigley's heart drummed fast as he walked up to them. Should there be violence, they were strangely organized in a way in which the girls would get hit too.

"Because having me around would remind you of it too often," he began calmly. "Everything you use to lie to yourselves to."

"Like what?"

"Money and looks."

"You think we're rich?" said Zera. "We bring brown bags to school."

"Relative to him, Zera," said Debby. "Gosh, don't be such an insensitive bitch."

Rickward laughed hard at this.

"I do say now, where's the caviar?" Cory joked with a posh accent. Zera started laughing with Rickward. Carrie walked over to them and raised her eyebrows at him.

"So what do you use then?" she snidely interjected. "Why did you swim out of the ocean instead of going for truth?"

"You played truth or dare, Carrie?" asked Cory.

"I dared him to swim out as far as he could or tell me the truth about his accent."

"And I said I'd tell you when I got back," Rigley completed.

Carrie scoffed at this, welcoming his sarcasm. The shadow of the canopy danced fast over them as the tree branches rattled from the summer gust.

"You're all geniuses, really," he continued. "Writing my name in to Zionée's team. Afraid of how much less of a chance you stood at beating her without me?"

"Afraid of you, obviously," snickered Debby.

"No," said Rickward. "We like that about you. If you think about it, we're not sabotaging you. Isn't it great that we can help you break such a tough stereotype? I mean you should own it. It's groundbreaking, Rigley. You're like the first in a new species. A Super Asian."

While their lungs lost every ounce of air from each building insult, Rigley clenched his hand into a fist inside of his pocket.

"Like, we're just sad bullies inside because we're... so intimidated by you," Debby cracked up as she held her sides in pain. Zera tried her hardest to laugh with her lips pulled in because she had a cut on her lower lip. She giggled melodically and evilly.

"Well, if you didn't already have a reason to be."

Cory and Rickward instinctively pushed forward, protective of their girlfriends, and ready to beat him up and get away with it looking like heroes. Rigley smiled.

"You've done so much for us already," Rickward said threateningly. "Why ruin such a beautiful friendship?"

"It could get real ugly."

"So make it," goaded Rickward.

The drumming in his heart raced his hand against the second. But before Rigley could complete the arc of the first punch, someone's hand had caught his wrist just when his fist was inches away from his mouth. Cory flinched a little and quickly looked around to make sure that nobody saw the handsomeness in his face turn yellow. Rickward quickly backed out of the way. Rigley turned to see Zionée standing next to him, her hand still gripping his wrist. She glowered at the snobs before smiling defiantly and saying something in Japanese.

"Are you speaking weeaboo?" asked Debby.

"I'm speaking like an alien from the planet Earth. It's nearby. And I said," Zionée replied, pointing to his fist. "See this? This is our secret weapon," she said pointing with her free hand at the fist.

Rigley was dumbfounded.

"It carries the spirit of our team. I was always afraid of giving up my feelings to the likes of you and I thought that by destroying mine it would make me stronger. But I came just in time to keep him from giving you his because... as hard as it is for me to admit it... it is just what we need. You can't have it. Our team is going to take its rightful place above yours – without cheating – without expensive AP tutors – and without raising our hand once against your all too deserving faces. We're going to break your smiles the proper way."

Zionée let go of Rigley's hand and he dropped it and blinked, not immediately registering what was happening to be real or not. She turned to him and smiled with the same pride he predicted her to suffer.

"Because we're a team."

Edin joined in closely alongside them, his eyes lit off of the torch in his sister's, their determination ignited.

"And we believe that giving us Rigley is going to be your biggest undoing," she told them. "You're all about to meet a real Super Asian," she added, pointing her thumb at herself.

Rigley and Edin nodded firmly to Zionée's words. Rickward and his friends laughed on a short, light tempered note, hiding their rage and indignation. Then they turned and headed back to their quaint little tree at the center of the mound before looking back as Team Omega walked away.

"Hey, that was pretty cool what Zionée did, sticking out for Rigley like –," Zera spurted, unable to help herself.

"Zera, you so have a thing!" Debby joked.

"No, I –"

Debby's face suddenly darkened with the very tone of her voice.

"Don't ever say shit like that again."

Rigley smiled as they walked towards the stairway leading to the large, wooden doorways of the main building. Edin was shaking with a new sense of humor trembling throughout him. Zionée shook her head, still tingling a little herself, she took out a bag of Pocky from her pencil case and handed one to her brother. Then she held one out to Rigley.

"Don't worry," she smiled, her voice still trembling nervously. "It's not eyeliner this time."

6 – The Stairway Debate:
Zionée vs. Debby

Tessa walks back from the cafeteria with a camcorder after recording more footage from another fight. Her video montage for her sociology class project continues to grow. She takes a good look around to make sure that no one is looking before descending down the hidden staircase behind the science building. On the lowest basement floor under a maze of noisy pipes of steam is the small corridor leading to the now awesomely changing mural. The multicolored, intricate letters carefully interlocking unbolt to new secrets of the public social world. Tessa puts away her school-rented camcorder, remembering not to let any of this slip into its feed, as none of the teachers are to know about this place. Moving a brilliant, yellow bandana around her neck up over her mouth, she sprays a new message on the mural in red and purple ink.

She continues to harness the power of the graffiti mural beautifully. The days of trophies and gold-sealed certificates are on a far rolling shore; receding into a horizon she didn't look back on. By organizing all of the worst gossip to turn all of the smaller groups against the powerful ones, her maniacal ambition to create a new status quo is starting to take form; one that is not ruled by power but by the strength to stand up for those without it. The school hierarchy, as they know it, is now under the forecast of a powerful new wave of change. In class, many of her classmates previously shy or bullied silent are now fearlessly sociable. She notices many of them walking to the cafeteria lines during lunch rather than paying to have someone line up for them. But there are always those who did not get the message, and from this ignorant crop, she films for material out of her latest homework project.

Later, Tessa and some friends walk down the hallway drawing looks of condescension from some high-nosed kids sitting on ledges with anvils for books. The privates look at them with study-worn eyes, heavy with the intensity of advanced placement level work. They overhear them talking about how much easier they have it with their normal level curriculum. Tessa notices Alonzo and Emilio averting their eyes up at the mirror pane below the corridor ceilings. They can see their reflections in the glass fossilizing under this gaze, as though they are becoming normal in an out-of-date way. With the hierarchy so different, Tessa now hears from more people talking about being nurtured under the painful indifference of their parents and teachers. As they come to school every day to a system that knowingly cast heavy locks around the limits of their potential, they constantly bear the underestimating weight of their invisible chains.

At the end of the hall, she stops by the windowsill, nodding at her friends to go on ahead. Tessa sits down on the sill and touches the faint, purple splatter of stubbornly permanent marker on the glass. The small graffiti stencils the student body, moving about in ever-shifting entropy, oblivious to its disintegration. From this height, it is difficult to perceive any disorder or segregation. She takes out her camera and looks at how little memory there is left. Tessa nods with decision: It is time to take it past recording schoolyard fights.

When she gets to class, the teacher instructs them to make Venn diagrams for two different but similar social issues. Tessa's hand awkwardly guides her pencil to make the shape of two overlapping circles. A kid sitting behind her starts snickering at how thin the space is in between.

"Tessa, that does not look like a Venn diagram," Alonzo says with a vulgar humor to his voice. The whole class laughs. A girl with curly, black hair and a ponytail giggles in her direction before going back to studying. For some reason, playing the routine of having her assumed-to-exist balls busted in front of this person feels unusually real. After class, Tessa waits to watch her leave before punching Alonzo in the arm.

"What was that for?"

"*That does not look like a Venn diagram*," she repeats mockingly. "What was that all about?"

"Chill, fool. It's not like you're not used to it by now. This is how it is. This is how we talk to friends."

"At times it doesn't feel that far from how we talk to the ones who aren't."

"So? Some people just got more lemons in their hearts to squeeze."

Tessa laughs at this. They walk out of the class with the remainder of the students getting up from their seats. As they enter the hallway, she searches immediately in the glass pane for somebody.

"Man, it's just normally I would've said something back. But something stopped me from thinking."

Alonzo breaks out laughing hysterically after he notices her pretending to look up at the glass.

"Oh, that nerdy, quiet kid Janet?"

"What did you say?"

"What? I just said –"

Tessa looks at him dangerously and he steps back a little.

"Cool it with the language okay? What the hell is that? Don't call her that word. She's just trying to study hard and go to college and pull her family up in the world. She does not need that ancient label to –!"

"Dang, all right," Alonzo mutters. Tessa looks around as several people's head spin to their direction. She hears a thin, high voice giggling and turns around. A handsome boy is actually the one making Janet laugh. He also happens to be wearing specs. Tessa chances a peek at her locker and sees the car keys dangling from it.

"Don't seem like they need that much pulling up, though," says Alonzo.

As Team Omega continued its unanticipated, meteoric rise over the next couple of weeks, the principal's academic competition was finally gaining traction and receiving some publicity from the campus news. All of the other teams started to recover their motivation. Racing forward from the momentum Rigley's improvement brought, more than ever before, they began to mobilize as one. Zionée dismantled a few extracurricular clubs she didn't attend in order to concentrate more time together with her teammates. At soccer, her teammates noticed she was no longer just giving orders. For the first time, she was giving praise. After beating the varsity team of a rival school, Zionée announced that she was quitting mid-season to try out for track. She got tips on how to get into the school track team from Hashim and Zera, both of whom were already on it. In the library, Edin and Rigley practiced speaking quietly through playing chess. On these occasions, Rigley rehearsed most of his jokes with him to test which ones would be funny in class.

Vicky continued to visit them at school to check on how they were doing, taking time off work and school to do so. After drying her hair off from a water tennis match, she entered the main hall where she saw the other team counselors gathered in front of the digital scoreboard. A tall, preppy student with shoulder-length hair walked up next to her.

"Hi, Vicky," said Joshua. "You just get here?"

"Yeah, I don't have to class today."

Suddenly Ronna appeared next to them and Vicky gulped, sensing she still might remember hijacking her ride home.

"Sup Vicky."

"Ronna," she winced. "Hey."

"That your team up there on the board in fourth place?"

"Yes."

"I thought Omega was meant to go last."

"Do you remember mentoring?" Joshua chuckled. "When we were still students here?"

He gave Vicky an accusatory glance.

"Yeah, yeah," she smiled, keeping her cool. "I do."

"Didn't you almost," Ronna said. "You know, get kicked out of the program once because you were so out of it?"

"I remember the reason why," Vicky said patiently but vindictively. "But abandoning your classmate so that you could follow some stupid rule about snacks kind of put what I had to do into perspective. So if you can imagine it, I did learn something worth passing on."

Suddenly there was a blink in the scoreboard and Team Omega switched spots with the third place rank that was Team Epsilon. A couple of the counselors gasped. Ronna and Joshua gave Vicky a congratulatory look of approval and she nodded back courteously. But then there came another beeping click and blink from the board and the scrolling digital font of Team Omega was now switched over into second place, right below Team Alpha.

"Woohoo! That's my team!" Vicky laughed breathlessly. She then raised her eyebrows smugly in response to their now dumbfounded, speechless expressions before walking away, twirling her water racket.

After sneaking underground to check the ever-updating forum of graffiti, Tessa is tempted to destroy the whole balance of the school hierarchy, if only to engineer a scenario where she can save Janet and come off as a hero. The futility of past attempts to catch her attention agonize her. Every time they make eye contact, Janet glares at her from across the classroom. At nutrition, Emilio explains that she keeps an online journal for school reform. On the site, Tessa finds it to be littered with entries about what a dangerous, psychotic delinquent she is. Instead of coming off as a social revolutionary, she gives the impression of being another gangly punk that gives the publics a bad name. Before she can lift the spray-can, Yogun grabs her wrist and stops her.

"Hear you been acting funny," he says calmly. "Like you're infatuated or something."

She pulls away but doesn't let go of the can of graffiti.

"Don't abuse it," he warns. "That's not what it's for."

Tessa blinks before lifting her eyes up at the giant, complex pattern of hues her brain fights to photograph anew each time she is here. She sighs and hands over the can. Yogun takes it and puts it in his backpack.

"Looking cool for somebody else, wanting to be the hero, getting a girl's attention. All of these ways come back to you. It's how it always starts. People. Corruption. Popularity. But what about your friends, huh? Your classmates? When you got power, you're not allowed to think of only yourself."

Tessa nods, idly unwinding and rewinding her bandage wraps several times over her hand. They are silent for a moment but the apology is there. Her heart, heavy with learning shame, lightens at the sight of something. She spots the new, green colored paint from some of the public gangs corruptibly in league with privates.

"What's this say again?" she asks, pointing at a blue squiggle of words.

"Public clubs suck."

"Do you believe that?"

"Well yeah, they do," he shrugs. "But I'm not much of a club guy myself. I bet even in the private sector, all they do is meet up, have lunch, and collect names on a sign-in sheet."

"In that case," Tessa says. "It looks like there's one for creative writers. And I just happen to know one."

She bolts off with a map to her madness flashing clear in her mind.

"Yo, where you going?"

"Following the rhythm of her rage!"

The bell rings and lunchtime starts. As usual, she knows where she is when she can see the brilliant glare of light on the glass line atop of the smooth, white lockers outlined in blue. She drinks in the contrast as she catches her breath from running so far and fast. After briefly checking to see if there's any dirt on her face, she slips quietly into the writing club where Janet is supposed to be. The cabinet is a posse of fashionable privates sitting in an isolated corner of the English room having lunch. A couple of new members are awkwardly sitting and waiting for something to happen in the diurnal tank of a classroom, empty of creative thought. Janet, determined to not be exactly one of them, is writing poetry by the corner desk where it is not lit by the ceiling light.

"About last week," Tessa starts as she takes a seat next to her. "I was defending that kid."

Janet sounds wary and continues writing, not looking at her. She finishes her sentence and then drops her pencil down loudly.

"No, you were defending you," she mutters, biting off a snack bar and talking with her mouth full. "Not what you think you stand for."

"Well, maybe if you gave me a chance to figure out what that is," Tessa says tersely.

"You mean other than through beating people up? Go ahead. Innovate."

She stares back at her for a moment and then looks back down at the paper on her desk with a few lines of poetry. Tessa watches her mouth muscles moving fast as she chews and senses the limit of her patience approaching.

"Can I have some?"

"No."

"What are you doing?" she asks her.

"We're writing poetry."

Tessa looks at the other socially unglamorous members of the club sitting idly like they are waiting for class to start. None of them are writing or even talking. Then she looks to the other side of the classroom where the same posse of girls are sitting around the teacher's desk, playing cards and reading the cotton ratio of their scarves and sweatshirts.

"You mean those white girls over there?"

Janet takes out her pocket mirror and holds it up.

"Did you forget?"

Tessa smiles. There is also at least one Indian-American girl among the group with a face and personality readily evolved for popularity. Tessa taps her fingers on the rim of her hat.

"I wasn't talking about their race. I meant the color of how empty they are inside."

Janet blinks for a moment and is unable to help but laugh at this.

"You sure you don't want to join?"

Tessa looks around at the nearly empty classroom and then back at the club cabinet. They are now eating lunch.

"Hey," Tessa calls at the cabinet. "Hey!"

They glance airily in her direction while still absorbed in their conversation about gelato.

"Hey! I'm talking to you!"

They look up at her dirty, disheveled, battle-ridden appearance and hold in their laughter with trembling smiles. The leader, a girl with bright, brown hair and dark, blue eyes, starts smiling slowly at her.

"Yeah?"

"Sign in sheets are over there," her pretty Indian friend says.

"Thanks," Tessa says, going to the sign-in sheet pile and taking all of it.

"Hey, I'm talking to you," they mock as soon as she turns around.

As they laugh, Tessa leaves the classroom for a brief moment and then returns with a sonic grenade full of things people with minds narrowed down to mainstream, pop culture make fun of others about. The invisible device thrown from her hand detonates into a musical renascence of super synthesized J-Pop and passionately, colorful heroism until it becomes an explosion loud enough to blow up the silent monotony. Out of this sterile, barren hangout spot, Tessa pulls its quiet, shy introverts, full of hand-me-down, off-catalogue attire, smudged glasses, beady faces, and outcast body types. From this point on, in every club across the school, all the miserably idle kids get up to follow this brave, exotic sound.

Zionée's headache about how Tessa Seredin revolutionized clubs throughout the school grew and worsened. It had been a part of a renewed campaign amongst her classmates, who were getting resentful of her approaching return to her old throne. Although a few of the other teams were more laidback and friendly. Hashim and Edmondo focused hard on averaging out their collected GPA's into a decent score and struggled to balance the time they studied for their AP's. Like Team Beta, Team Epsilon was also very mutual with Rigley, Zionée, and Edin. Letitia's team was always grateful to accept help from them. And after becoming better friends, Rigley became more careful about the Tessa Seredin rumors around his teammate. Zionée was rumored to be muttering in a possessed trance sometimes when she got things from her locker. By sneaking up on her one afternoon, he heard what was actually her lip-syncing to the Japanese Pop music playing in her earphones. When she started the chorus, expecting to be lonely of the male vocal as usual, she was surprised to find a well-timed harmony from behind her locker lid. After she closed it, he was already gone.

Zionée and Rigley finished their reading at the same time for English class. Rigley turned to Letitia and Hashim. Their conversation whistled through Zionée's ears while she looked at the colorful Japanese Anime characters decorating Rigley's binder.

"Hey, last class, were you laughing at what I said or at me?"

"I can't remember," said Hashim.

Letitia giggled.

"Well, can you?" Rigley asked earnestly.

"No, I can't remember either. Were we Edmondo?"

"You're asking me?"

"You're all so funny," Rigley said.

Zionée removed her earphones and hid them under her mantle flap as the bell rang. She started quietly humming the tune again while looking at Rigley anxiously.

"All right, Tammy let's hear it!" he shouted excitedly.

Professor Tammy arrived late for the first time, unusually. In her class, whenever somebody arrived late or was turning in their homework in the last minute they would have to improvise a rap. Rigley, who was often the victim of this rule, delighted to catch her at breaking it. She put her book bag down and removed her glasses and began beat boxing to her own beat. Her rap was simple and elegant, masterfully improvised from incorporated themes of Milton's *Paradise Lost*. Everyone applauded and laughed, briefly amused by the small tickle of something interesting happening in class before the actual hard work of the day's lesson plan. Tammy then had Rigley help her pull the blinds up a little, allowing the bright, crepuscular sky to illuminate half the classroom as she turned on the lights for the other half. As they analyzed the new text, finally moving on from Milton, they started discussion for the next book, which focused on a boy's obsession with his mother.

"Can anyone give me an insightful reading of the subtext?" asked Tammy.

"Oedipus Complex!" snapped Debby quickly.

"Good. But I mean investigate why he primarily uses jokes attacking people's mothers," Tammy patiently rephrased.

"Okay, wait," Debby said, asserting more mental power into maintaining the spotlight. "I think it's because he's a dick."

Tammy chuckled.

"Nice one, Debby. I'll let you know when I give out extra credit for humor."

"Yeah, because then you'd know when you get deducted," Rigley said.

The class groaned and laughed at this.

"Settle down, settle down. That was my burn," she said, turning to him. "Rigley, you're always doing that. Can't you participate for real?"

Several classmates nodded with agreement and parroted her.

Zionée read over the text again and became too still to blink. It would only be a matter of time before someone brought up a correlation to her and Tessa Seredin. Tammy's eyes fell on her expectantly. After several minutes passed, everyone remained silent. Zionée kept still and sustained her eye contact with the chalkboard.

"Because he can't quite get over his sense of abandonment," Rigley suddenly spoke.

His exasperated classmates turned in their seats to look at him. Tammy nodded cautiously, waiting for the punch line.

"As children, we all remember that first day of school where we're dropped off. It's terrifying. To be suddenly torn from under the eyes of our mothers. The character here has an affinity for 'yo mamma' jokes because – perhaps like most of us…"

Zionée's eyes widened as far as they could for her pupils to almost be round.

"…Perhaps like most of us, he never quite got over that sense of abandonment. The mother who picks us up on that first day suddenly becomes a different person to us from the one who dropped us off."

Everyone was quiet.

"Cool," Professor Tammy finally said. "Very cool."

A few of his classmates looked surprised.

"And by the way, finally," she added, causing another small gush of laughter. Rigley turned and noticed Zionée staring at the back of his neck, which was getting red, which consciously caused him to cover it with his hand.

"What?"

"All right," Tammy resumed, adjusting her glasses and flipping the page, "can anybody tell me the literary device that the author used in the text to create a vowel rhythm?"

"Tammy, wait," Carrie said. "I think I got a pretty serious answer to support Debby's claim on it being an Oedipus complex case. You don't mind if I use a contemporary analogy, of course."

Before she could continue, to everyone's shock, this time it was Zionée who raised her hand.

"Oh, am I substituting for math today?"

Zionée turned for a second in Rigley's direction. Whether the twinkle in his eyes meant that he was making fun of her or if he was giving her a look of encouragement, she did not know.

"Alliteration!"

"…And how?" her teacher asked.

"Awkwardly assisting!" Zionée said really fast, "And such phrases with repeating beginning vowels or consonants."

Tammy nodded approvingly. Rigley chuckled a little. Zionée looked down at her desk. She smiled secretly to herself. He was brewing in her.

After school, Zionée waited under the bright, mid-day clouds, for Edin in the courtyard. The area was half-enclosed by the left wing of the main building and is perpendicular to the gothic bell tower. The statue nearby was freckled by the light stencils of leaves from the tree canopy. It stood on the edge of the square patch of grass next to the classroom windows. A large, oak tree was divided into reflections in the panes of glass and shadows on the brick walls. When Edin arrived, Zionée was watching a flight of blue jays return to a nest of eggs perched in the highest branch. She stole a look at his reaction, sensing that he was feeling the same. The birds were protective and nurturing and had flown great distances to return. Tessa came to them through rumors and vicious gossip, which was no place for a child to reunite with the parent they had never known.

"Come on," she said. "Let's go home."

The next day, Zionée faked sickness at the nurse's office, left with the thermometer, and broke it to use the mercury to make a rare carbonate. Professor Weavins had his students brew up difficult chemical substances to use as hall passes. The more complex the solution meant the more permissible the excuse. While Weavins was still scratching his head as to how this chemistry was possible, she pulled Rigley out of his desk by the hand.

"Before I let you pull my most prized student out of class," Weavins said with his dry, Australian drawl. "What is it I'm excusing him for?"

"We have to go do some hardcore making out," Zionée replied breathlessly.

Rigley looked at her as he glowed red from the large ripple laughter and hollering this stirred from their classmates. Zionée smiled. She and Rigley ran down the hall and headed towards the old lab where they changed classes from a semester ago.

"Hardcore what?" Rigley asked.

Edin closed the door behind them. Zionée made a noise that sounded like an anxious squeal as she whipped the top off its string and then began spinning herself in sync with the rotating seat of her chair. She was breathing fast and loudly like she was starting to hyperventilate.

"Hey, calm down! What's wrong?" Rigley asked, forcing her to a stop by grabbing her shoulders.

"Stairway debate!"

"You? You've been nominated?"

"And Edin's going to be debate recorder."

Sheltevue had a judicial system of electing students to debate popular issues on the stairways of the main building. The student with the greater jury approval would get to skip a step up the staircase. Their classmates would stand against the wall as the jury, the volume and strength of their applause determined who would advance and who would not. The one reaching the top first wins the debate. It was no coincidence that the system was born out of the way privates rushed to class between passing period, skipping a step up the stairs and leaving their friends behind in order to get to the best seats in class. Principal Flores often walked on the far side of the stairs closest to the wall to keep from getting run over on her way back to her office.

Rigley offered Zionée the water that he considered dowsing her with to cool down. The issue she was elected to conveniently polarized them on opposite ends of the scale. It was regarding academic favoritism, and Rigley felt as much at home on the overlooked end of it as Zionée felt on the favored end. Once again, Debby and her teammates have entered one of their names into a situation they did not volunteer for. Zionée quickly started winding the string around the top again.

"If I win the debate, Tammy, Nairs, Xen, Weavins – all of them will hate me!"

"Well, Weavins hates everyone, so you're safe there," Rigley joked. In a burst of frustration, she ran out of the classroom and he didn't see her for the remainder of the day.

"Want to spin the top?" Rigley asked Edin light-heartedly. He nodded and started rewinding the string.

Zionée was pacing up and down the hall beside the empty staircase later that afternoon when Rigley found her. Though she had a strong, athletic control of her breathing when she ran for track, at that moment she could hardly stop her lungs from contracting. When she saw him standing there, she stopped and looked at him before turning back to the window. Rigley remained still and quiet while she was turned away. She saw his transparent reflection disappear as the outside light changed. When she turned around, he appeared next to her, holding out a folded piece of paper. It was a speech he had written for the debate. She looked over it and read it at light speed, looking up at him strangely and greedily several times. When she was finally done going over it the second time, she looked up at him again and he appeared more alien than before. Then she turned away again, thinking it over quietly.

"Verbatim."

Her eyes moved back and forth at him with a nervous indecision as she bit her thumb.

"It'll be like theater!"

"Or Anime!" Zionée shouted, turning to him with an enthusiastic craze.

Rigley smiled.

"Or Anime. But in English. It's like... different language, same passion. You know like the opposite of voice acting."

For Zionée, memorizing things was something she trained all her life to be as capable of doing when it came to tests and quizzes. But none of it required any of her emotion.

"You mean like how voice acting – they read off the lines pretending to be the characters?"

"Yes, except my lines will be reading off of you."

"The character pretending to be me?"

"That is, I'll pretend to be you."

"But you'll speak through me!"

"Right!"

Zionée stopped and remembered something.

"But they'll notice I'm only saying your lines if it hasn't got my feelings. It's like we speak different languages. I mean come on – who could be more different than you and me?"

At the same time, both of their eyes lit up and they smiled.

"Different language, same passion!"

"I'll speak in Rigley!" said Zionée.

"With Zionée's feelings!" Rigley completed. With hope burning in their hearts, ignited by the exciting absurdity they saw in each other's eyes, they began training for the day of the debate.

Tessa runs over to the newly launched Graffligraphy Club. She grabs the sign-in sheet and is again happy with the result. Then she runs back to the Karaoke Club; again, more names from both publics and privates. On the school campus news, the reporter speaks enthusiastically about the upsurge of new clubs that are engaging and active in contrast to the exclusive "hangout" spots that are the private clubs. The students in her Karaoke Club look up on the projector and watch her interview Janet in an online video stream.

"Thanks to Tessa," Janet says while blushing, "The public clubs have innovated the club system into something new. He's caught on to something. Clubs aren't places to just sit down and listen to one person in class. I used go to private clubs and it's always about one ego."

"So what's it like at one of Tessa's new clubs?" the reporter asks.

"It's like being brought back down to earth," Janet gushes. "With the feeling that everyone else is there too."

Yogun sits down next to Tessa at lunch by a patio table, as she is about to eat a cafeteria sandwich.

"Damn, Tessa, you bold."

"I'll take my chances."

"I'm not talking about the sandwich. The privates know who you are now."

"The whole school knows who he is."

Tessa almost chokes when she sees Janet standing shyly over their table.

"Sup girl, how's your brother doing?" Yogun asks.

"Keeping out of trouble," Janet says, her eyes not leaving Tessa. "Hey so, Tessa, I hear your grades in anthropology could still do with some improving."

Tessa swallows the bite and almost forgets how to talk. Yogun looks at his young protégé's face, now fluctuating between blue and red like a siren berry, and laughs.

"They could," he answers for her.

Yogun pats Tessa on the shoulder as he gets up and leaves. Janet sits down and takes out her study books.

"Is your face ever without a bruise?"

Tessa blushes.

"It's how I stay literate," she says. "I'm actually good at anthropology. Tracing human ancestry is a hobby."

"Oh, yeah?" Janet smiles. She pronounces "yeah" in a cross between the way Canadians and Hispanic girls sometimes pronounce "yeah". Janet moves in real close to Tessa's face. "By the way, I have some suggestions on how you can change up your creative writing club. But on the whole, I think you've done it a lot better."

Tessa smiles, grateful for her approval.

"Well, you couldn't have said it better than that cute girl on the campus news."

Janet laughs, blushing at this.

On the day of the debate, Zionée arrived at the stairwell, finishing a stick of Pocky she had nervously been keeping in her mouth like a cigarette. Professor Tammy walked up to her and asked for one. They had a small laugh explaining to the others slowly arriving that they weren't smoking. All of their English class was excused for this event. Tammy walked aside to leave it up to the speakers to coordinate the debate. Hashim guarded the stairs to let people know that an official debate was happening and that they had to forsake the convenience of going up or down this flight and head on to the other one.

As Edin tested his recording microphone, Eslamida asked Zionée if she was ready.

"Oh yeah," she replied confidently.

"Where's Rigley?" Edmondo asked.

"He's home sick," she said.

"Wow, how supportive," said Debby. She walked past them to where her friends were. Zionée glowered at her before turning back to her other classmates.

"He's here," she told them. "He's here," she said one more time, looking to the top of the flight where Edin was testing the debate recorder. The window behind him shined with the light of the previous day, which she followed her reflection into.

On that very same stairway, Rigley zipped down the rail and crashed. Zionée helped him up, holding her laughter in as much as she could.

"Could you please –," Zionée broke out in little controlled bouts of laughter, "Stop… making me laugh!"

And then she punched him in the gut.

"All right," Rigley wheezed. "Let's go over it again."

Debby took her steps up the flight first, facing everyone on the opposite side with a smug look. She tossed her pack of gum at Zera to catch.

"Students are encouraged to try harder if they feel their efforts are rewarded," she started. "If we don't give a reward to those who are exceptional, then we're not being democratic, are we? Should we limit ourselves to the custody of everyone's feelings rather than the potential of a talented few? I mean, hard work is important. But if a teacher sees an exceptional spark then why shouldn't they give that person an extra push?"

About five or so of them nodded and applauded. Debby took five steps up the flight. She gave Zionée a sly smile.

"The debate now calls representative of the refuting party, Zionée Dunnelin, to step forward and speak," said Tammy.

The emotions of her being trapped on that beach boiled up but when she closed her eyes thinking of who else was looking out through them, she calmed down.

"Your points are valid… to a degree," she began.

"You're not going to get to the top by agreeing with her," Edin thought. A girl looked in his direction; did he say that out loud?

"But what's it to you?" she continued, gathering strength and volume. "Like me, you can be expected to get the right answers and make the teachers feel like they're doing their job. While you might not consider yourself stupid, you probably know what it's like to get the answer wrong."

"Wrong?" Debby started. "I'm never wrong. And just because our grades are similar doesn't mean you can speak for me."

Tammy made an "ahem" noise and took the microphone momentarily from Edin.

"Just to be clear, while this debate is named *Zionée vs. Debby*, in the style of Supreme Court cases, your names represent issues larger than your own personal feuds."

"So you never ask yourself if you were wrong either? And that's the problem isn't it? None of us ever asks ourselves about what it's like to be the one counted on to fail. To be the mistake everyone gets to learn from. To be the one rooted against."

Rigley clapped. It was just the two of them and Zionée took the line he scribbled down at lunch on a napkin and made it new. His clapping continued to echo in her mind as she continued to speak out against the disgusted look on Debby's face. Zionée rose up the steps as her classmates start to cheer, advancing her way up.

"I think you shouldn't waste time asking yourself what other people think or feel like because that's not what getting ahead is about!" Debby shouted. Everyone booed and she stomped down the steps with disgust.

"I used to think that. I sometimes still do. It doesn't make it right and it doesn't make us different. But what does make us different? Getting better grades? Making it to state championships? Everybody here – including myself – has confused being different with being better."

She looked at Edin as he held the microphone close. Then she took a deep breath and turned towards the window at the top of the flight, waiting for the shade of bright golden, yellow that lit the glass up just enough to restore its reflectivity. She moved until her reflection was in the spot that it was the day before so that she could follow it back for a moment.

"Rigley?"

Zionée was sitting on the stairs. She moved down a step and sat next to Rigley so that they were on the same level.

"Why do you always wait? I mean nobody really waits for you."

"You do."

"Only after you stood up for me that one time in class. And it's not like we don't end up sitting next to each other in class anyways."

"Skipping these steps… is such a distinctly private thing to do."

"You're not a private?"

He ignited the look in her eyes with the mischievous spark in his own.

"I've never felt like one. Testing into this program has felt as easy of a mistake as being put on your team."

"Then it was a beautifully miscalculated one," said Zionée, gratefully.

Their smiles wore comfortably on their faces until they faded under the slow gravity of contemplation.

"There's something else. I can't do this without you telling me about," Zionée stopped. He looked at her, bemused.

"Tell you about what?"

"About her!"

"I…"

For an incredibly awkward interval of time, Rigley didn't speak.

"…know. You're not the authority on who Tessa Seredin was anymore than I am. But for some reason, I feel like I'd believe it the most if I heard you say it. Listen, I know I've acted like I didn't want to know."

Zionée looked off and rubbed her eyes briefly before blinking.

"How can I not want to know? I mean really? You think I wasn't tempted sometimes? I mean… she looks! So much! Like! Me! Why are you wincing?"

"Ha, you're intense," Rigley laughed lightly.

"And I'm an orphan," she said quietly. "All I'm asking is if… you can help me know how it feels not to be."

Rigley smiled, a sudden confidence in her possessing the light in his eyes.

"Yeah. Yeah, you could be. You very well could be."

Zionée beamed at him and stood up and he was gone. She found herself surrounded by her peers at the stairway debate again.

"Everybody, including myself, has confused being different with being better. If I stand above these steps, then I will be noticed above the rest!" her voice boomed across the corridor as she stood on the second highest step, nearly reaching the top. Debby sunk against the wall, feeling defeat already sweeping over her.

"But if I forget the steps I took. Then I'll forget that I have known what it was like to be no better than the rest of you. Favoritism is based on forgetting that. I won't forget. We are different. But we are not better!"

Everyone broke out in applause and cheered. The cacophony of their excited praise filled Zionée's heart. For a brief moment, she caught sight of it. The shadow of a blue jay returning to her nest flashed across the golden patch of window light on the floor. She and Edin hugged happily and then she slid down the rail, catching everyone's high-fives. The last one she caught was twenty-four hours fresh in the memory of her palm.

2nd SEMESTER

7 – Tessa and Tesla

Tessa squeezes a patch of faded purple on her cheek with a small pad of alcohol. She spits at the mirror and rinses her reflection with the dirty sleeve of her worn, tattered jacket. After finally hitting it off for two weeks, Janet is decidedly not speaking to her again. So she beats up a couple guys that are acting like they need a lesson on what it's like to feel victimized. And if it is to her misfortune that one of them is Janet's cousin, Tessa might aspire to think a little clearer next time. During nutrition, she smashes her chocolate milk carton, splattering its contents all over her and Yogun's clothes.

"Okay, warn me next time before you do that."

"He probably told her how I beat the crap out of him and his friends and made me…"

"You did."

"Me! Look like some kind of – some kind of bully or something!"

Yogun laughs and calmly wipes his cotton sweater clean with a napkin and starts tracing over it with a stain remover pen.

"Well, if you tough enough to enjoy it. Ain't you?"

"I am tough enough. But I don't enjoy it."

"Not even a little."

"No."

"Then there's the problem isn't it? You start thinking too much."

"What do you mean?"

"Fool, why do you think them little freshman be cussing you out behind your back? Because they got big brothers who can mess up anyone who tries to do anything to them."

"So what are you like my big brother?"

"I'm saying when you are at your most desperate, how can you tell yourself you are any better? Using all that green you paid to doctor up your advantage like that? And still, I had faith in you. If I were going to pick someone to lead this gang to its demise, it would have been someone who's only beef was over a girl and didn't see anyone worth fighting for other than himself. There'd be toughness, for a while, yeah. And when you got so much of it that you distance the people on your side, it becomes an asset to the people who aren't. But you got the gift in your loneliness, Tessa. You got the gift to see it in others and do something about it."

"Thanks, I always did have a high self-esteem when it came to being a lonely loser."

Tessa touches the sports wrap on the back of her hand.

"That's not what I meant," Yogun laughs. "So listen, you want to prove to this specky little girl you're a man, you do it on their turf, show them you understand. But remember it's got to be bigger than that right? Because she won't be the only one watching you when you do it."

Yogun takes out a notebook and starts writing some rhymes for the slam poetry club. Tessa is silent. Although she is moved, looking at all the friends and classmates literately communicating their pain and daily grievances, she still doesn't have a clue about what to do to make Janet forgive her.

As she got off the bus, Zionée shook her head at the cold morning's brutal touch and breathed a visible sigh of respiration. She put on a black jacket around her stylish Japanese sailor shirt. Letitia walked by and nodded up at her.

"Nice outfit," she said before going to join her friends.

The weather had finally begun to cool. The gothic castle rose high in her view against the damp, blue sky.

After winning the stairway debate, all of her peers began to treat her with greater respect than before. One thing she was particularly relieved about was how her teachers didn't hate her.

Although the debate had her elected on to a position to persecute them for their favoritism, they took it, on that rare occasion they showed that they were, like adults. They were careful to not play favorites as much and took more into consideration the previously less outspoken classmates. Professor Weavins still made fun of his students. Professor Xen was still too nice and a pushover with grading curves. Professor Nairs was still incurably sarcastic at every lecture. Professor Esparanza still ate in class when no one was looking. And Professor Tammy continued endorsing an environment where there was no absolute sense of a right answer. It was the getting to part that her lesson plan usually stressed.

Meanwhile, Edin was struggling to adapt to the new waves of affection coming from his older sister. In finally accepting her connection to Tessa, she had done her proud. But the question of his heritage continued to be met with fewer answers. He did not have anybody like a parent to do proud. His growing anxiety started to mentally broadcast visions in his sleep; dreams where Tessa found them both and only recognized Zionée. In the subtle onset of these sleepless thoughts, there was a new seed of rivalry that was finding sustenance from his nutritious envy.

Rigley sat down in front of him at their usual table in the library and they played a few rounds of chess in order to practice some conversations.

"You're awfully quiet today," he said in his dryer winter voice.

Edin blinked.

"You were making so much progress. Has talking to that girl you like in class helped yet? What was her name?"

Four vowels. It was only that. When Edin tried to mouth the name of his classmate, he was again haunted. The face he saw in his sleep lurked behind his lids in any given blink. In their gaze, all the sound that respired from each measured inspiration became lost in a vacuum. Rigley took his knight with a bishop. This exposed his king to Edin's queen.

"Your checkmate. Go on."

"Checkmate!"

It was a whisper with an almost discernable sign of vowel sounds. Rigley smiled, satisfied with having caught the decibels.

So many weeks had gone by where he couldn't bring himself to win and would let the game continue.

"Good progress," he said. "Now if we could only think of a way to get you to eat in school too."

Edin took out his uneaten lunch and offered it to him. Rigley shook his head.

"Edin, why did you stop talking?"

He stared back at him for a while until Rigley thought he wasn't going to get an answer. Then his phone vibrated and he read the text message.

"When did I start?"

Edin nodded. He mouthed "your accent" and breathed out the phrase with a slight hint of sound. Rigley looked back, as if ready to trust someone for the first time with a secret so painful and dark. Not many people were around.

Tessa throws away the towel and avoids the look she knows she wants to give herself in the mirror. As she washes her hands, she starts contemplating the possibility that she may have condemned herself into an abyss with no way out of the heart she took to learn in its breaking.

School fights are a miserable matter. Nobody else's heart rate climbs as high as the ones that get caught up in them. When over, the proud, tattooed, and tattered sink back down into a depressing slump of shame and guilt. Tessa sees a girl with a bandana who everyone teased for smelling so violently athletic. The bandana girl starts throwing bits of eraser at a shy, quiet girl studying in the corner.

"What are you writing?" Alonzo asks. Tessa is finishing up a notebook entry in preparation for her sociology project.

"You know that thing you said about the lemons in our hearts? People are like lemonade stands, man."

"Take it out on who you can. Everyone's buying."

"Simple enough," she says. "You've read Socrates?"

"I like knowing how to pronounce him."

"Well, I've never read Socrates," Tessa chuckles. "But I like knowing how to pronounce him too."

"I think Janet over there would like to hear you try."

Tessa looks up and drops her pencil audibly. A few seats away Janet is reading a book by the philosopher. When she notices her looking, she turns away. Janet turns the page even though Tessa could tell how she hadn't finished reading it.

"She still mad about you beating up her cousin, huh?"

Tessa shakes her head.

"Wouldn't you be?"

"Honestly, man? No."

"You ready with your assignment materials?" he asks, taking out his notebooks and taking out a spare pencil he keeps tucked behind one ear. She takes out her camera and nods. Tessa recalls the first time she starts to figure out what kind of sociology report she must hand in. After swiping Marco's camcorder one afternoon and playing take-away, the lenses accidentally land on something. It is the looks on their faces, not the ones in the fight, but the ones watching. The way their eyebrows pop, their mouths gape in awe, and their arms flail excitedly.

After the other students go up to give their presentation, it is finally Tessa's turn. The sociology teacher, half-impressed with what she is trying to do, stops giving in to the pressure from the PTA to keep her from using real fight footage. Students from all of his classes come in to watch Tessa's little films. The images bounce off of the projector reflecting several gross close-ups of bruises and cuts, all of the battered blues and lyrics of red. No other series of school fight videos posted on the net receive as many views. In her editing, her voice, and sometimes her direct point-of-view of the action, she captures a rhythm in what most people cannot understand. But at lunch, they stampede across the campus in massive hordes just to watch a couple of kids have the worst day of their lives.

"It's called the Genovese Syndrome," Tessa says in the middle of the silent montage of her latest fight. Suddenly, for a brief two-second interval, sound returns. The screams are animal-like, possessed.

"And it's not what we have," she continues. "Out there, we have something else. We're bloodthirsty fans."

The sound continues to return in increasingly longer intervals until it fully synchronizes with the video of the boy getting pummeled to death by two large, older students. The screams of the crowd alternate with his cries of pain. A girl in class stops snickering and winces. Tessa deliberately plays with the relationship between their two senses of hearing and seeing, filling up the mirror of their minds until they break from all the pain they reflect. Witnessing became experiencing, until finally a girl leaves the clubroom and then gradually, one by one, they all walk out.

Only a couple kids linger, friends of the bullies. The tallest, shaved-headed one with earrings is Janet's cousin.

"What's your deal? They were just trying to teach the kid a lesson."

"That justifies it, huh?" Tessa snares back.

"Hey foo, calm down. Look we know we can't take you. Same basic mentality."

Tessa grips her fingers tightly in a fist and then loosens them. She is beginning to forget the teacher is still in the classroom and that as long as their discussion remains verbally diplomatic, he doesn't have to call the police on her again.

"We don't mess with you because we know you can stand your ground. So we respect you for that. That kid needed to learn respect."

"You and your friends provoking me until I lose it? If you ask me, you have a very sick and pathetic idea of respect."

"It ain't our idea. It's just the way it is. You're there. Doesn't have to be that complicated. I come to school everyday on Wednesdays. Know why? Because nobody else bust my balls on Wednesday. On Wednesday, everybody is busting Larry Ikler's balls. If he wants his respect, if he wants his safe passage through Wednesday without feeling like he wants to shoot himself by the end of it, he has to fight for it. I mean we don't got no sports. We got the worst books, teachers are always out to get us, and our clubs, whatever you may think homie, are now the joke of the school. So what is left for us? How else are we going to get respect? If we don't even have that, we have nothing."

Tessa doesn't breathe for a moment. The more of a point he made, the angrier she gets with herself. She starts fighting her urge to beat them up and prove that they are wrong and that she is right with all of her refined weeks of street fighting skills; but she instantly gets how this will only serve their point further. So she let's go of her breath, touches her eyebrow, and then swipes the eraser dust off her table with one idle hand.

"Leave the privates to me."

"What can you do?"

"That's my business. As for you. Your codes and your respect – you know what? You've got it all figured out except for one thing. There will always be someone who respects or disrespects you. You're just using the word as an excuse for survival without ever having the courage to find out if there are worse things at stake than your own pride."

"What the fuck do you know? That stupid kid I beat up was badmouthing my brother. Yeah, everybody's got the guilt of it here. Who are you, huh? You probably talk a lot of shit about people too!"

"I haven't!"

"What do you call your homework assignments, huh? Oh, you so immune to hate then because you got no one to love! That's why Janet avoids you. It's pathetic, man."

Not knowing what else to say, Tessa moves to turn off the projector but changes her mind and leaves it on. She grabs her things and walks to the door.

"Excuse me, young man," says the teacher. "Class isn't over."

"Hey," says the thug, with the same obnoxious tone of nonchalance. "All I'm saying is – he had to be taught a lesson."

Tessa turns violently but doesn't move past the teacher's desk. Then she shoves a model globe off the table before storming out the door.

In the bright, chandelier light of the hallway on the main building, some students moved aside from the tournament scoreboard, hanging like a giant domino with flashing pixels. Rigley walked up to it and looked up at Team Omega's place on it. The digital lights scrolled high above the others like a blinking train station destination.

Number two.

He felt the glass trophy cage within his finger's touch now that he had fallen slightly to the opposite side of it. With this unsteady new throne, which his self-esteem had ascended to, his heart became heavier with the weight of far more responsibilities, evolving out of the dark.

"Wow, look at that," said a mischievous but impressed voice. Principal Flores had appeared next to him, tucking a small pen behind her ear that could almost be mistaken for a hairpin. "Think you can take each other to the top before the end of the school year?"

"I'm more worried about not taking anyone down."

"We haven't spoken much since freshman year," Flores mused. "And I'm proud of the reasons for that."

"Not as much stuff to confiscate. I don't bring my skateboard as often anymore."

"Oh, your skateboard, you're so bad," Flores sarcastically mocked.

Rigley laughed and she chuckled too.

"But it's cool you know what you want to do in life so early. Whether it's drawing with lead or urethane... preferably not using school property as the canvas. By the way, did you finish scraping that gum under Behring's tables?"

"Yeah," he chuckled.

"Yeah, you better."

"Still feels alien to me. I get quiet now in class when everyone's talking about their grades. It used to be so easy to make fun of them when I didn't care. But now I have the trust I've been given to not screw up."

"You just got to learn to juggle a little between dreams and ambition."

Flores turned around and gestured at the other students moving about.

"So what if what you want to define you is a little different than what they want? That doesn't make them better than you. Or am I getting the point of your speech wrong?"

"No, I guess not," he smiled.

"And this is the highest grade point average you've yet to achieve."

"It is," he said.

Flores caught the look on his face.

"So what else is?"

Rigley smiled and shook his head. They were both quiet for a while as the talkative noise of students passing by melted around them.

"I was put on this team to sabotage Zionée and Edin," he suddenly said out loud to himself. Flores looked at him and blinked. "Do they ever make fun of you for it, Flores?"

She squinted at him suspiciously.

"For what?"

"How good or bad the ones you put your faith in can make you look."

"Comes with the territory," Flores admitted shyly. "Teachers and students."

The slow, reverberating notes of the electronic bell echoed across the hallway, accelerating the tempo of the crowd around them.

"See you, Flores."

"Hey. Try not to screw mine up too."

The principal looked at him peculiarly as he went on his way and then faced the digital board again. She sighed and laughed breathlessly. It was working.

On his way to class, Rigley stopped by to get something from his locker. The pale, diurnal light from the window at the end of the hall shimmered across the smooth, polished floor. Reflections of students quivered and dissolved into shadows.

"Did you do last night's reading for English? I need the notes!" Zionée called from a few yards down the hall. New friends and teammates one typically accumulates from doing sports orbited between them, all with an agenda for her attention.

"Hey Zionée!"

Zionée smiled at each one of them but kept bouncing glances back to Rigley. She kept to moving closer and keeping their conversation going. Every time Rigley looked up at the mirror line above the lockers, expecting to see her disappeared from going off with some friends, she remained and was actually moving closer to his reflection.

"Hi!" she said with extroverted charm, "Did you take them Cornell Notes style?"

"Hey excellent race last Friday!" another kid complimented.

"Thanks," she breathed but again turned forward. "And I'm hungry!"

"Hey thanks for the two dollars!"

"No problem," she smiled, and was now next to Rigley's locker, which she moved the lid between their faces out of the way. "By the way, I need somebody to make me laugh."

"Try your face," Rigley said.

"Tried, but yours is funnier," he said.

Zionée was navigating through her growing new popularity with a clumsy disinterest. It was the first time Rigley had ever made a friend where belonging to a sports team or an extracurricular organization did not interrupt her time or desire to be around him. At lunch, they met Edin in the classroom of one of Zionée's old clubs.

"Edin told me about how you've been trying to get him to talk. And after hearing that it's been working…"

Zionée took out a new square chessboard patterned dish and began mounting it with their sushi.

"Ready?" she said with smiling light in her eyes at Rigley. "Gambatte!"

"Yeah, hold on."

He took out a box containing large, thick-rimmed yellow sunglasses and gave them to Edin to put on.

"Oh, man, what are those?"

Zionée bit her lower lip and started laughing as they magnified his eyes under two large, yellow squares. Then they started the game.

When it was after school, Zionée and Edin waited with Rigley for his bus before going back on campus to retrieve the yearbook they've been storing alternatively in each other's lockers. As they flipped through it, looking through all of the old faces, they found it odd that the names were scratched out.

"Ha, this looks like Professor Xen… oh man, what if that's Nairs next to Tammy?"

Finally, she turned to the page where Tessa's face was, smiling up at her like her own. Zionée turned the book a little, tilting it for Edin to see but also to appreciate how peculiar she was. In spite of their physical similarity, they almost seemed a world away because of how much more honest her mother's smile was.

"I keep seeing her in my dreams," Zionée said to Edin.

He placed the yearbook back down before looking up at the empty bird nest in the tree nearby, gripping the skin of his backpack. After the shade had moved, they walked over to the ledges outlining the school's front courtyard. She put the yearbook away and took out her notepad instead to show him her artwork.

"I've even made a drawing of her, see? Not as good as Rigley but I'm getting almost... right?"

He nodded approvingly at her Anime drawing of Tessa but had trouble hiding his discomfort from the increasingly uncanny resemblance of it.

"For now, it'll do," Zionée grinned.

Edin looked away. She really was visiting them.

"You want to hold on to it for me?"

He took it and hid it deep in his multilayered folder.

"So I'm glad you're starting to eat," Zionée said. "If your chess skills are any indication, you might even grow another inch."

They took out their empty lunchboxes and started eating the crumbs out of habit by picking at the corners.

"It's not fair that you should have to starve through lunch when everybody else isn't self-conscious of what they eat."

They overhear some kids walking by complaining about the size of their new shirts because their parents are always trying to save money buying them ahead of their growth spurt.

"Yeah, it's so normal for them, isn't it?" she continued, after reminiscing. "To get to go through all that with their parents – even the worst of it is something we could envy."

Edin had the same look. Their particular foster parents were more like business clients. They finished picking all of the crumbs. She looked up, noticing the blue jays in the nest. He did too. They had returned and grown, almost unmistakable from their parents.

"Edin. You're old enough for me to stop treating you like my little brother. I mean well because... I'm your friend. Like, I am. Always here."

She laughed at herself and then went to go see if the bus had arrived yet. Edin was not sure if she meant to sting with him with those words. She voiced it with such sweet promotion but to him it sounded like a complete demotion; Less than family, less than siblings, and just friends. That night, where for so many hundreds of nights they would brush their teeth in front of their mirror with the light dimmed, Zionée spat out her toothpaste and flicked the dial up to the brightest setting. Edin wanted more than anything to know what she had. But she was not sharing the certainty with him. The certainty of being someone coming from somewhere and to know it and not be afraid of what the light illuminates.

In less than a week, the same thugs, including Janet's cousin, gleefully start pushing around a small, bowl-haired kid with glasses near the cafeteria patio. Eventually they provoke him into taking swings at them for their taunts about his mother. When he breaks the laughter out of one of their jaws, they get defensive and, out of the nobility of defending an injured friend, start to attack him all together.

"Are you sure about this?" Alonzo asks as Tessa pops in a new tape into the camera. "What if they try to slap the camera out of my hand again?"

"Just record it and stay at a safe distance!"

Alonzo knows by now that they have violently different notions of a safe distance so he stays to the side as the crowd starts to gather and uses the zoom feature instead. Tessa finally starts to understand what Yogun has been saying. It isn't about being able to prove to others that she is right so much as it is about showing what is wrong to others. She is constantly fighting herself not to intervene in every scuffle, thinking that there is always a balance of fairness tipping somewhere in the underdog's favor. Her self-righteousness makes her both a frequent target while also enlightening her on the complications that violence produces. Sometimes both sides are equally vile and completely wrapped up in their hate. Sometimes the one who gets hit first takes vengeance for his ego too far until he trades places completely with his predator. They delight in the power of their own pain and start to enjoy seeing its recreation in their predator-turned-prey. But Tessa is now liberated of any intentions to be a symbol of vengeance. She isn't anyone's avenger or savior. She is one of them only so far that she is a symbol for her self, protective against all that threatened what that constitutes. And right now, it is the people she believes in.

Tessa kicks down at one of the thugs she flipped to the ground and uses the other one as a shield from the attacks from Janet's cousin. She misses one and is kicked in the leg, causing her to stumble and fall backwards. As she recollects her balance, she senses her success in allowing the previous prey to get away. To her horror, the bowl-haired kid steps over his glasses and joins the crowd cheering the violence on. She picks up a cafeteria tray to block but they knock it out of her grip. The crowd grows dense around them, as the litter-ridden asphalt arena gets smaller. Suddenly the chanting slowly changes and the sound waves register a different set of words than what she expects to hear. At first it seems like she is imagining it. It starts growing louder with what seems like bloodthirsty excitement but as the crowd starts swarming threateningly around them, she senses the strength of their indignation amplifying with their numbers. A couple of large, quiet kids reach in with powerful arms and one of them succeeds at pulling one away. Another pulls Janet's cousin back before he can punch Tessa again. The chanting is now almost deafening as the other two cronies stop and turn, becoming self-conscious. It sounds like "fight" and then it blurs and blurs until one lone voice distills the rest of the chorus with harmonious clarity.

"STOP!" Janet shouts.

"Stop! Stop! Stop! Stop!" the crowd dangerously shouts, their voices collecting in strength and volume. Tessa peers through a black eye and to her amazement, gone are the impressed faces of awe. In their place are angry and judgmental looks most popular kids waste on making the weird ones feel insecure. It is over.

Tessa breathes with excitement and relief. The thugs all walk away, trying to keep their tough composure but against a quarter of an already overpopulated school population, there is nothing left to show for. They win the fight. Their opponent is on the ground. And in the next couple weeks they can keep their respect and nobody will mess with them. And in spite of that respect, people now know what insecure and pathetic victims they are of their environment. Tessa, who had no plans to win the fight, gets up off the ground after taking a soft, small hand. She looks up and it is Janet. For the first time, her classmates and friends are helping her up and escorting her to the nurse's office instead of the police officers.

In the cafeteria patio area, no one claps, no one cheers, and no one says a thing. One by one, they quietly disperse back into their groups as though nothing had happened. Alonzo puts down the camera when one of the larger kids glare in his direction. They are coming out of the dusk of a new meteor but not entirely so different without the shame of what made them passive before. United on a feeling of injustice they tried to ignore, they are now better prepared to come together and forget that they're all strangers in the face of something they all know wasn't right. Yogun walks up to Alonzo who is sitting on the table with no umbrella.

"I don't think he means to turn that in this time," he says. "Safe to say I'm right?"

"Safe to say."

Alonzo shrugs and puts the tape away.

In the school library, Rigley made boxing gestures as if re-enacting a Dicky Eklund fight. The sepia windows filtered in a little light from the black and white sunset outside.

"And she swings with an uppercut to the jaw!"

Zionée rolled her eyes and shook her head. She closed her book.

"Look I don't think she –," Zionée wanted to say "my mother" but wasn't ready to say it aloud in public, " – was the sort who would do that."

"Okay, stick with your bourgeois view."

"Agreed, and you can have your social superhero."

"I like the sound of that."

Zionée blew a raspberry until the spit from her tongue fell in Rigley's eyes.

"How about that?" she joked.

Rigley wiped his eye and doused her with the remaining drops in his juice pouch. They started working hard to forget what was still tickling their funny bones and to retrieve their concentration on the Renaissance. Zionée closed her book again and interrupted Rigley.

"I mean come on! How would she even pass off as a boy?"

"People do it all the time. Look at Eslamida."

"Eslamida just has short hair and she isn't a lesbian!"

"You don't have to be a lesbian to do passing. What if you were just born the opposite way you felt?"

"Oh no. Goshers, Rigley. What are you telling me?"

"Goshers, Zionée, didn't you know?"

"What is the opposite way you feel?"

"When I'm around you? Sane."

She smiled and then took a sip of her water, looking at him. Then she turned back to her reading. Ever since she started embracing the Tessa legend, the idea that the mother she never knew was all these amazing things got her more open to talking about it with Rigley.

"Why are you so inclined to believe in her going undercover?"

"Because it's what I would do if I had a twin who got expelled and I had no other way to redeem who he was."

"Well. I could never even imagine sacrificing an entire school year for something like that."

Rigley smirked and wrote in some new notes in his binder. Zionée watched his face as he worked.

"Was it for community service?"

"No. She was expelled. It had to be on record that she was."

On their way to class, Edin was getting so sick of this topic that he broke off and walked behind them at his own pace without their noticing. Rigley looked back a few times to make sure he was still there.

"I just can't see it. Okay. Then what was her name? Of her new identity?"

"Tesla was the black sheep of the family."

"I just can't believe I have an uncle too. Maybe you should go into I don't know – whatever profession involves," Zionée raised her eyebrows dramatically, "Tracing people's ancestry."

"I never said I know it for sure. Why do you like to risk my word for it?"

"It's because of your imagination," she said, stopping and looking at him.

"Overactive?"

"Sincere."

Rigley smiled at her and they were quiet for a moment.

"Still makes me wonder," she said. "Why everybody else thinks of it in so many ways."

She looked at him for a brief moment, curling the corner of her mouth into a curious smirk. "Besides, the whole undercover thing? I just can't see why you'd make a choice like that unless it was to benefit anyone other than yourself. I would never allow myself –"

The bell rang. Their eyes popped. Professor Xen, who was also one of the Track coaches, was already running up the corner of the hall from the stairs.

"– To be late!"

They dashed down the hall to get to the door before he could beat them there and mark them tardy. Even as they rushed by, Rigley savored the shiny, white metal lids of the new lockers, the glassy clean floors, and the unstained windows. On the third floor, where most of the private classes were, they really had their own infection of purity and exclusivity. A little worried that the school may one day receive enough private funding from the rich parents to turn it into an actual private institution, he felt the urge to graduate as soon as he could before that happened.

They met up after their last class and decided to go wait for Edin in their secret lab. At the doorway, Zionée searched her pockets for the keys.

"Rigley, do that trick again."

"Left pocket?"

She checked it and there was nothing.

"Nope. Oh wait, we're fine. Let's just wait."

They put their backpacks to the ground and sat down against the wall.

"You gave him the keys?" Rigley asked.

"Duh. I can always trust my brother."

A shadow of guilt slipped over Rigley's face. Zionée noticed the brief wrinkle between his eyebrows and scowled at him, thinking he was mocking her. He smiled back. Zionée got a text message before she could ask him what it was about.

"It's Vicky. It says. Ugh. 'Hey are you two going out?'"

"Of our minds," they said at the same time, before laughing.

"I mean, really, if we had a dollar every time we've been asked that lately..."

"Yeah, I mean it's totally," Zionée agreed. She touched her chest, trying to convince herself that the heat inside was normal when he was around. "Like it is just – that kind of – that you know – like – it is just... so..."

"Okay, now say that in Japanese," Rigley said. "I'm sure it'll make sense then."

She tried and he amused himself correcting her. After a couple minutes of silence, Rigley ran his hand through his hair. Zionée turned to him, moving a hand and plucking a single strand of white from it.

"Do you not eat your five a day?" she teased.

"There's another story to that."

"Not the same as your accent?"

"Nope," he said, quickly changing the subject. "Do you think you're being a little insensitive?"

He continued to speak, uttering every word with a difficulty that stretched the Englishness of his accent until she started to really appreciate the full oddity of every vowel sound.

"Have you ever thought about what it means if only one of you has a photo of a parent who looks exactly like them?"

Zionée laughed, a little distracted by picking out the pattern of his eccentric speaking accent. "Edin and me were adopted at the same time. So Descartes, where do you take it from there?"

"That Tessa may only be *your* mother," Edin thought as he stared at their surprised faces suddenly apprehending his presence. They stood up and allowed him to open the door with the key.

"Hey," Rigley greeted. He tried to tell Zionée not to talk about it with his eyes but she didn't see as she walked past them both and flickered on the light switch.

"I could never go undercover," Zionée said almost all too soon.

"What, you mean like being a spy?" Rigley feebly joked. She put her things down and finished her Bubble milk tea.

"No, I mean like Tessa."

Edin's ears perked up with a frustrated curiosity; what was it now?

"No, I'm serious. I don't look anything like Edin to pass off as him. We're not twins. Look at us."

Rigley was quiet but passed a few worried looks at Edin.

"Aww," Zionée said looking at her watch while spinning in the chair. "Track meet. Got to go, later guys."

She grabbed her stuff and ran off. Rigley looked at Edin, who was staring straight at the wall. The only sound meeting their ears was the ticking of the clock in the classroom.

"I want to be alone," he mouthed as loud as he could. Rigley nodded silently and left to give him his space. The concept of twins was a harmful new thought. Now there was twice the evidence that he didn't look like their only known relative and that he might be adopted from a different set of parents. He was left alone in the dark and forever filled with the emptiness of not knowing while Zionée at least had her ghosts.

Edin opened the cabinet and took out the chemicals. He found ones labeled with his own name and blinked for a moment. Heating up the beaker, he mixed the solution and started scanning the elephantine problem covering the whole of the page. Under the light of the little lamp, he continued to boil up the water in the beaker. He titrated the substance and punched in the calculations, correcting his work feverishly along the way. Could he still love Zionée like a sister even if the frighteningly inevitable revelation that they were not related at all should surface? Edin wiped the sweat from his forehead, beginning to dread the answer he would get. The chance to prove his lineage and his sibling bond to the only family he's ever known suddenly became as fragile as the moment. All those years of cram school and skipping grades and AP prep classes had put his mind out of gear with his body. The more he discovered how much alike Zionée was to Tessa, the more he started shaking with an impatience with himself.

After finishing the experiment, he calculated the answer and wrote it down. Then he checked the odd number answer key at the back of the book. He was quiet for a few minutes, waiting for the numbers to change before his eyes like a mirage. Then there was a lot of glass exploding against the wall. Suddenly his phone vibrated in his pocket. Zionée texted him to let him know that she was returning. It was her favorite beaker with a little Anime character of a fox demon decorating it. He scrambled to clean it up but the chemicals were too hot and dangerous to touch without gloves. The heat arising off of the floor warned him not to get too close to the acidic sting of the pH level so he quickly went to look for something to clean it up with. In the backroom, he found some clear, blue dental gloves and hastily put them on despite how they were too big for his hands. As he took a broomstick to sweep up the glass, he heard the doorknob turn. Zionée came in, panting in her track hoodie. The rapid rate in which her breathing decelerated made Edin dread that she had already seen what he had hoped she hadn't. When he came out of the backroom, she was looking down at the shards, each containing a colored fragment of the Anime character.

"Look Edin, I finally got it!"

Coming in out of the next second's blue was Rigley, juggling three beakers. He saw Zionée and then clumsily reacted and dropped all of them. Zionée's eyes were murderous.

They fought and didn't speak to each other for a whole week. In the meantime, Edin hung out with Rigley and was learning fast how to un-mute every word he could think of to ask him why he put his friendship with Zionée on the line to cover for him.

"You know, it could just be psychosomatic. Your throat muscles. Mentally, you've got some kind of lock," Rigley began, though Edin suspected he wasn't totally invested in what he was saying. Then he cleared his voice. "It was just a beaker right?"

Edin looked down and then nodded slowly. Rigley took out a small, black sketchbook full of Anime drawings. They looked a lot like them and there were individual ones that included him. Edin looked at his Anime style reflection with an odd interest.

"If you won't give it to her, I'll understand. It's yours to do with as you please."

Edin nodded, taking the drawing booklet. It was already dark and cool outside but despite not layering up, Edin felt warm again. When he got home, he took it to Zionée's room. She was power napping and breathing angrily in her sleep as though from having a nightmare. Edin woke her up and she opened her eyes slowly. She flipped through the booklet and her eyes, which were like cold glass, softened.

"I guess I'll get over it," she said with a comical punch.

8 – Super Achiever

In the singular light of his sister's CD-player disc lamp, Edin shuffled through the many detailed drawings of Rigley's sketchbook. The Japanese Pop CD whirled like a trapped paper windmill inside the fluorescent case, which had a special glass that redirected the heat to the metal so that the audio parts remained cool. It was one of Zionée's favorite customized inventions and done so that she could illuminate her workspace and listen to music at the same time. The air was lightly riddled with the jumpy melody of an opening theme tune from one of her shows. He had turned the volume down so as not to disturb their foster parents. In the many afternoons he shared with Rigley, Edin watched the patient fire burn in his eyes as they mirrored the carvings of his mind. He could see not a single reflection of wonder or fear for what was going to happen next.

Was that what it meant to know what one wants to do in life?

Edin looked at his Algebra 2 homework, organized economically before him from the easiest to hardest problems. Despite the mental monotony of the labor of numbers and variables, he often didn't look at the clock much to see if he was finished. But when he got to the seventh of the fourteen-problem set, he became frustrated enough to stop. He looked at an eighth grade class photo where the top of his head showed just behind a girl, being the only one shorter than him, standing in front.

The next morning, Edin peeled a line of clear translucency through a moist and misted window and looked outside from within the moving bus. From the condensed part of the window, the world seemed to move slower, obscured by a thick, cloudy blur. Through the newly cleared translucent line, it was as though a smaller piece of the world was streaming at a faster speed than the rest. That was where he needed to be: on the other side of that line.

He had always seemed to belong more immediately to tomorrow. His generation was rented to it more than any that came before them. From their parents to their teachers, they were encouraged by both the disappointment and praise of others to take on responsibilities light years ahead of the ones that the previous generation took. The entire core curriculum of the school known as advanced placement motivated students to time travel into the future and take courses out of their college careers in order to get ahead and relieve themselves of a few flaming rings they would have to jump through. Some of them, like Vicky, were even fortunate enough to leap through an entire year's worth. As a grade skipper, Edin had been doing this since middle school. He took all of his sister's hand-me-down books, even the ones that weren't required by school, and read through them all. Secretly, he struggled harder than his mental capacity could sometimes absorb and never betrayed a second to stop learning ahead of his class. But in fighting against the miles between themselves and this mysterious Tessa Seredin, he and Zionée now had differing agendas. By the time he got off the bus, the condensation had returned.

The classroom glowed brightly with its usually ultra-bright interior lamps melted ambivalently with the exterior daylight. Only in days of damp, blue skies did the contrast become as striking as the light of an asylum interior. Edin was quietly working on homework assigned that day while gradually leveling a coffee cake to crumbs and finishing the always slightly bitter orange juice he suspected took flavor from its plastic carton.

"And then he was like, 'Oh? Well yeah, your face is something' blah-blah-blah complicated metaphor," said Debby. "And then she was like... trying to insult me back in Japanese again."

Edin's ears perked. He found their laughter to sound not unlike a mean bark. This was his only class with mostly sophomores.

"Such a creep, right?" chuckled Cory.

"So weird," added Rickward. "What losers."

Edin's face grew hot with a rush of blood that was coursing fast in his temple as he gritted his teeth. The corner of his eyes was lightly tattooed with their multicolored, stylish clothes. They were standing in their lazy postures as if they owned the world. The ones who sabotaged them and left them stranded on a beach a hundred miles away didn't know when to stop. They continued tearing at the honor of his friends to shreds with a remorselessness outfitted to those growing up with very few consequences to educate the tooth and claw of their play.

"And Rigley," said Zera. "I don't want to know what nature he's freak of but it certainly isn't ours."

Everybody around her laughed approvingly. Edin slammed his textbook down loudly and the noise from their area halted for a moment. He didn't care if they heard him. They snickered in his direction as he furiously scribbled something down. Then he walked up to them.

"Sup Edin?" Cory smiled with the same tone he used to charm girls. "What's chilling, little man?"

Edin glared at them. He slammed the paper down. Cory took it but didn't read it.

"I don't know who you're trying to kid, but I don't swing that way."

"I think he's saying you like your bros a little more than your hoes," laughed Rickward. "You like that Edin? I got him for you."

Debby and Zera cracked up but Edin's face remained stony. Cory glared back at him.

"Well, which way would you like to swing? I won't discriminate."

Edin shook a little from his rage, swarming inside him. It became harder to stay still in one place. Debby swiped her curly, blonde hair out of the side of her face.

"Neither will we," she said teasingly. Zera looked around her friends for cues on how to act next.

"I think he's angry," she smiled.

"If your friends were being talked about badly behind your back, you would be angry too," Rickward said with obnoxious sarcasm. "Have a little empathy, Zera. Is this why you're here, Edin? You want to say something to us?"

Edin thought hard but he couldn't construct anything fancy to parlay his wit like Zionée and Rigley did. Rickward cupped a hand to his ear.

"What's that? What's that about my mom? What did you say?"

He turned aggressive and took on the feeling of being offended. His friends all played along with it. Edin didn't like how quickly he panicked under Rickward's mercurial flex in emotion. They all started laughing viciously.

"Ha, we're just kidding around, bro. We're sorry. Okay?"

"Or are we?" Zera asked.

"Zera, shut up," Debby said.

"So sorry," Cory added. Edin shook his head, curled his fingers into a fist and bit his lip preparing to curse loudly into the trap that they were setting his vulnerability up for.

"Hey, what's your problem, Zera? You weren't at the study session!"

Edmondo, Letitia, and Hashim appeared behind Edin. Rickward and his friends dropped their sarcasm, now going on the defense themselves. All of their fake smiles instantly faded.

"Hey don't talk to her that way," Rickward said threateningly.

"Oh, have a little empathy, Rickward," Letitia said with her German accent slightly protruding with her anger.

"What, for your people? I'm a little confused as to which."

Cory and Debby snickered meanly at this.

"That's not funny!" said Hashim. "Zera, come on. You can't keep hiding your grades from us or we can't average our team score."

"I'm sorry, I was just studying with Debby," Zera squeaked.

"Debby's not on your team," Edmondo continued irritably. "We are! Remember? We didn't even want you on it. Flores put you with us because your so-called friends wouldn't let you be on their team in the first place!"

"Hey Edmondo. Why don't you shut up about that?"

"Hey Rickward. This is none of your business!"

"I'll make it my business!"

"Oh, I forgot. You're right it is. Then take responsibility for it!"

"I am not an 'it'!" Zera shouted as if only to participate. "I'm not some object to take responsibility for!"

"Then stand up for yourself instead of relying on these jerks to do it just so they can trash talk you whenever they want!" said Letitia.

Hashim and Edmondo looked at her, impressed. Rickward and Cory exchanged embittered looks.

"You know just because Rigley made it cool to bash us –"

"Well, then that's perfect, isn't it?" Letitia continued, getting angrier. "Because it was all of you who made us feel uncool, so I guess we don't need the extra peer pressure."

"Yeah, if he didn't stand up to you, it was always going to get more obvious!" Edmondo added. "Always expecting everybody to laugh at your stupid crap in class! Some of us actually want to learn."

"Learn to piss off," Rickward sneered. Suddenly Hashim grabbed Edmondo's elbow.

"If Team Omega won't lose to them this way, neither are we."

"Yeah, we should chill out," said Letitia. "They're not worth it."

"Yeah, Edmondo. Chill zee heck out," Debby mocked.

Letitia gave her a withering look before turning to Zera and shaking her head with unapologetic admonishment. Edmondo sighed, softening in Hashim's grip. They all turned and started to walk away.

"Edin, come on," Edmondo called. Surprised at this sudden approval, he followed them away to the other side of the classroom.

Edin dwelled a lot on what happened that day, uncertain of what might have happened if Team Beta and Letitia didn't interrupt him with their problems with Team Alpha. Perhaps they weren't such bad people. Did Rigley change them all somehow? At the beginning of the year, nobody stood up to anyone. Since Rigley's friendship began with their team, his overall interactions with his professors and peers improved. He stopped clowning around as much in class as before. This didn't stop him from working hard to secure his position as the jest of the class. Like Zionée, everybody grew used to the annoyance he caused. His jokes weren't always funnier and smarter but he never made a crack at anyone but himself.

As for Rickward and Debby's crowd, things were on a decline. The deceleration of their momentum in popularity was beginning with the fewer rounds of laughter they received when they made fun of someone in class. Their classmates grew wise to the notion that the advantage of their popularity meant that half their battle was always over. There were still a few chuckles every now and then. But soon, even the teachers grew wary of their attention-seeking antics. Students of this ilk defined the privates. Their beauty and brains crowned the school's image in prestige and normalcy. They were the ones leading from the front line. They were not the hardcore partying drug addicts the media advertised anyone with clear skin and conditioned hair to be, nor were they exactly preppy. They were normal people who came to school with the expectation that they were the ones most responsible with making it look good and so deserved the rewarding delusion that they were better than the publics because of it. Though there were friendships between privates and publics, both sides diverse enough to have an affluent and popular demographic, on the whole, the snobs propagated an attitude that moved the public world far into the foreground of their attention span. But it was not in their nature to adapt easily to the feeling of being liked less than they needed to be without putting someone else down. Naturally, their jokes retreated inwardly and with fewer and fewer people in on it, they were soon alienating everybody. The snobs attempted to restructure on more exclusive terms of likability, a rubric that had become so intangible and insecure a notion that they were soon getting into fights with each other on the mound.

In his room, Edin stopped writing his paper at one point, distracted by something. He could still hear the insect echoes of the keyboard in his mind, the velocity of his fingers slapping the keys like raindrops pitter-pattering. To drown it out, he went to the foster family's old piano in the living room and pulled open the dusty cover.

Yes, this was it.

Something he enjoyed doing. Something he could use to deny thinking. The pressure of his fingers against the keys was light and timid, like his voice, at first. Then, softly and slowly, out of realizing his foster parents weren't home from their neighborhood ball the previous night, he played louder. At this very instant, every key, with each increasingly loud, glassy note, his mind was losing itself away from the grasp of something too horrible to utter.

It was his sister's fault.

He continued pushing the keys for brighter sounds, ascending to major scale but it was as if tripping on each note made him fall back on to minor scale. The very thought that he was running from started to run after him. It was people like Zionée. He shook his head and allowed the music to continue filling the air until there'd be no room left to think of it but the colors of sound swirling about.

"Yes, one day I shall be a musician," Edin thought. "And I shall not be related to her at all."

He stopped at the last, loud A-sharp.

He must have played for an hour. He began writing down the notes he improvised in the empty bars of the music sheets when he dropped the pencil. Edin stopped and stared at his obscure, shadowy reflection in the smooth, black glassy cover of the instrument.

Zionée was a snob. It was truth, as hurtful as it was innovative.

She was a snob of snobs, making her, in some ways, even worse. She had always possessed that ruthless sense of superiority even before she met Rigley. It was the feeling that she taught them how to survive on. Now that same feeling was what he discovered to be responsible for inspiring their very enemies. In spite of the stairway speech, Edin started to suspect it was Zionée's confidence that was the end result, not her beliefs.

They had to be better.

Edin could as easily count every note in the complete discography of The Police as he could recall how many times she told him that. He looked around at the wide, miniature atrium of a room where a loosely spaced galactic opera of dust was afloat. As though in each particle, he could see a dimension of a life different. He rested his fingers on the cold, polished wood. If maybe they weren't related after all. He dreamt of it. Free from the standards of perfection, so brutal an exertion. Of knowing how to run without the fear of being timed. Careless, and be fearless in that carelessness, like how Rigley was. To grow up and do the things he wanted to. No ghostly shadow of an uncertain relative to live up to.

When Edin opened his eyes, he found his sister sitting next to him. Her fingers rested on the keys but the depression of his fingerprints on the new coats of dust remained where they were and he knew why he hadn't been woken earlier.

"You've picked up music again, I see," she began. There was an insanely subtle quake in her voice and a heavy shadow under her tired eyes. She had been studying for the past 48 hours. "I opened your grade report. My bad, kid…"

She threw the envelope on the piano keys for him.

"I'm sorry," she said monotonously. Edin opened the letter and to his amazement and horror, saw a B.

"Our Team GPA fell back to number three."

There was a haunting blue light of a post-sunset dusk cast over Zionée. She stared past him, mirroring that possessed inner rage and terrible feeling of inadequacy. It was because they never had true parents to disappoint, that they had to emulate the disappointment in each other whenever one of them fumbled.

"I'm still figuring out how to apologize to Rigley," she said. Then she bit her thumb and shook her head.

"You know? You could help me," she said bitterly. "If you can figure out how to apologize to me, I could follow your example."

She stood up and left the living room. His eyes squinted to stay dry but he was so scared of the feeling pulsing wildly out of control inside of his chest. A sibling rage, uncontrollable and agonizing, threatened to diminish any sense of choice he had left in emotionally emancipating himself from her. He didn't care that she was older, faster, and stronger. He knew that he must make

Tessa proud. Edin brushed the music sheets off of the small easel, the flight of the paper flapping echoed loudly in the silence.

A week later, Sheltevue had a track meet. Zera and Hashim came in third and second for their respective track and field sports of pole-vaulting and running. Zionée was out of breath when she got to the end of the sprint, coming in first place. She continued walking and panting, taking no time to accept the praise of her teammates as she made her way to the locker room to get her stuff. When she exited out onto the field, there was an electric tension in the air. Vicky was waiting for her behind the front gate beside the P.E track and was leaning against the hood of her car.

"Hi," she smiled with those sleepy eyes.

"How are you?" asked Zionée.

Vicky touched her left eyebrow and gave her a serious look. They began walking for a bit together up the curvy slope of pavement leading from the bungalows to the science building. Professor Xen skateboarded fast down it on a bet to either skate the curve or give the curve. Zionée turned her head as he zoomed past to catch the paper airplane of her last chapter test that he threw.

"I'm terrific," Vicky said.

"Will we be like you?" Zionée asked. "When we grow up?"

"What?"

"Not answering our text messages and showing up suddenly, like a deep space explorer out of time. And knowing how to say hello without feeling the distance in between? Like a vacuum. It sucks."

"When did you learn to be so pretty with your hurting words?"

Zionée stopped to scratch her ankle.

"Will we be terrific?"

Vicky looked down and was silent for a moment as they walked. Zionée stared at the passing fluffs of light clouds moving high above them against the epic, cerulean ceiling.

"That's entirely up to you, Zionée."

"You came to ask about Edin, huh?"

They looked each other in the eyes. The school grounds were in a slow, fluctuating strobe under the passing nimbular shadows.

"About the team. You're all doing great."

"But not our best."

"Isn't it enough to finally have friends?" Vicky asked. "Is it worth this kind of attitude? I mean he was –"

She stopped and turned around at her, matching her eye level because of the elevated angle of the ground.

"He was what? He was what? You're not in our family. You don't know us. You're not even our teacher. You're just a kid with a job. What does it matter to you what he was or wasn't? Whatever that is, he can talk to me about. Not through some indirect channel because that is how stupid legends are born."

Zionée blinked and recognized her self for all of the anger her years of egocentripetal motion training had been holding off. Vicky took a step back for a moment and looked like she was about to walk away but didn't.

"And it's always worth the attitude," Zionée added. "Or have you forgotten? That's what it takes to stand up for what you want around here. And what you have to do."

"*Do* me a favor, then," Vicky said, her volume escalating to leap the distance she was putting. Her large, clef note earrings trembled as she shouted. "No matter how many people you hurt, so you can feel safe from yourself, continue forward and never reconcile. See where that gets you!"

Vicky started to storm away, down the slope to her car.

"Oh I will!" Zionée shouted after her. "Gladly!"

She turned around again and replaced the earphones in her ears and started listening to the music. It was a sad, slow Japanese pop song. As it grew louder, she could not hear Vicky running back up the slope behind her, shouting something. Although she already knew what she was trying to say, she was too angry to turn around and admit to her sarcasm.

Edin walked past the music room and heard the strumming of an acoustic guitar. Suzelia, his classmate, was inside practicing with such a devoted look on her freckly face that she didn't even notice him watching her from the doorway for the entirety of five minutes. He left the music sheets she lent him under the door and continued on his way as she started singing the melody from it.

It was sunny with the parting of clouds carrying a cool breeze that was too light to move the leaves. Sitting at the edge of the grass, Edin took out his sister's lunch. He had stopped wondering about why he was seeing less and less of Rigley and even his sister. It was a natural trend. The AP exam season was growing closer in the horizon.

"Egg and cress sandwich, how British," came a smug voice. "Did the accented one fix you that?"

He turned and saw Debby sitting higher up on the slope. The shadows of clouds as large as blimps continued to strobe slowly over the green gradation of grass. In the golden sunset, her blonde hair appeared dirtier but shinier. She moved down closer and he moved further. Edin turned to her and gave her a weary look. It was getting late and he was feeling uneasy.

"It must be nice having someone to talk to who could never talk back. Only listen. You can't imagine how difficult it is to get a word in with my friends. Especially Zera. God, won't she ever shut up?"

Debby smiled and read into Edin's gaze.

"You think I'm a bitch. And you're right."

She looked down for a moment at her fingernails.

"And you think I'm a snob," she said, shaking her head. "I can understand that. You come to school. You see hundreds of unpopular losers break their hearts against the poverty of attention people like me have to give. And I am the snob. But how is it the worst thing in the world to come here and not exist in the blink of a few beautiful people who don't see you? There are much worse things. Rigley knows this, that's why I would respect him if I weren't too busy hating him. But you don't know what a real snob is, do you? To be snubbed by your own blood, by someone you love?"

Edin didn't move but became increasingly fixated on what she was saying. Debby smiled and moved a hand through her curly, blonde hair.

"My brother. He always got what he wanted. Even when I was little he ignored me like I wasn't good enough to be recognized, like I wasn't good enough to be related to him, and he treated me like crap. I used to really look up to him. But looking back now, maybe the only thing that was heroic about him was how much he didn't care for what I thought of him. That killed me. But mom loves him. Always getting good grades – well duh, mom, of course he's better. He got the head start. You know how hard I try? How hard I study, how many games I practice for?"

Edin chewed and swallowed his sandwich. She seemed to be talking to herself for a while. Her voice was so bitter that he sensed this animosity was real and in some way, despicable. As the shadows grew over the grass, the last wash of daylight winked slowly to sleep through the tree canopy.

"And then everything changed. He fell in love. Got himself a girlfriend."

All of his things were packed but he had stopped.

"Happiest I'd ever seen him. He even started treating me nicer. As if that could begin to make up for it. But something else did. You know what that was? He lost his concentration. Messed up school. Sports. Everything. And then I took my chance to show mom what I can do. You know what she said to me?"

Debby got up from where she was sitting and slowly walked up to him until she got close enough to read the hunger in his eyes; the hunger to know what a mother would say to her child from the account of someone who had one. When she saw herself swimming in those large, boyish, bubbly eyes, she did not anticipate becoming a little sick with a sensation of pity and disgust.

"Good job. You're more my daughter than he is my son."

Edin went back to the music room, hoping that his friend Suzelia would have forgotten to pick up what he left for her. When he found the door still open with the sheets locked underneath the stopper, he sighed with relief before noticing how loud his breathing sounded. It was almost discernible. As he pulled the sheets from under the stopper and closed the door, he looked around. His solitude was secure. The music room was empty and it was already after school. He knew he'd have an hour before recitals began. He took out a voicemail that Suzelia once left for him during her choir practice. She had recorded herself singing by secretly calling him with her phone in her pocket. There was a male soprano with a really piercing voice in the mix. As the recording started, Edin took out the music sheet.

The clock ticked in a way that threatened to persist being the only sound in the music room. Edin swallowed and waited for the soprano section to appear again in the chorus. He had the music sheets folded out on the conductor's podium in front of him. It would be just like reading out loud from something. He opened his mouth, with the notes perched in front of him. His own reflection watched him impatiently from the glass wall on his left. He breathed in and the fear from all those times sound had failed to escape him clutched hold. The voicemail ended and he shook his head. Edin dialed again and replayed Suzelia's message. Still trembling as though he were being watched, he opened his mouth. There was a majestic quality to her, how nervous she sounded, and even amidst a group, how beautiful.

The soprano section started again. Edin locked eyes with the notes caged in the bars of the sheet music and opened his mouth, determined to set them free.

Tessa walks backwards slowly to behold it all. There are colors not used by any of the gangs turning the once intricately coded system into something mocking and clown-like with the gradient of a rainbow. There is hardly any legibility left in the mural. She shakes her head in disbelief at what she is seeing. Under the gravity of this disaster, she slides her back down the opposite wall. There is going to be total chaos and someone is going to have to take the fall. Did some stray gangster break in and mistake it for just another spot to tag on? She gets up and goes to her backpack to look for something. The language is unintelligible to their version of graffligraphy. She picks up the can, still half-full on the floor, shakes it, and sprays it everywhere, desperately trying to repair what she had last seen from memory.

"It's no use," says a grave voice. Tessa turns and sees the silhouette of Yogun descend from the upstairs daylight. "They going to think it was you."

"I swear, Yogun, I didn't."

Yogun shakes his head sadly. She can't determine if he is disappointed or angry.

"Do you remember who that new kid was? Way back at the beginning of the year? With the silly Italian newsboy hat?"

Yogun walks next to Tessa, and they both take in the damage.

"Look I can try to fix it —"

He shakes his head and takes the spray can back.

"You would have been a good rep. You would have been a really good rep."

Tessa looks down, masking her face in shadow. A minute of silence passes.

"I know it wasn't you," Yogun finally says.

"But you can't persuade anyone else of that?"

"You're not that good at school are you, kid?"

"What?"

Yogun's eyebrows frown upward. He looks at her with a guilty, apologetic expression.

"I spent all year guiding you to fly under my wings. But maybe all I've been doing was brainwashing you to play gangster with all my talk of changing this world. Playing tough. Letting you handle all the trouble so I could be working on my senior portfolio. If I was any kind of role model... Maybe you'd have done something different."

"No," Tessa says quietly. "I wouldn't have."

His shadow passes over her as he walks away.

"I have to go study," he shouts back one more time before he leaves.

Tessa slides down the wall with her back against it. Once upon a time, she remembers, she could say the same with meaning filled to the brim. All the letters behind her flow like an eternally broken rhyme.

After school, the next day, as Zionée was the last one leaving, Edin entered the classroom and showed her the crinkled paper duck of a B+ paper she had received in math. His silhouette was outlined in gold from the tranquil, solar glare of the evening pouring in through the windows.

"I'm disappointed in you."

She looked at him, confused. His quiet, choirboy tones arose from whispers at first. But then there was a deep lowness possessing another layer of it. Did he finally hit puberty?

"What?"

"I'm more," Edin began testing the sound of his voice as he continued to speak, "related to Tessa than you are. You brought the team down."

Zionée's mouth twitched from the infinitesimal moment of being thrilled that he was speaking quickly giving over to the horror as she realized what he was saying. Her lips fluctuated with growing difficulty between a frown and a smirk. She never imagined how painful it would be for her to finally hear him talk again. Every newborn word was a knife.

"We are related."

"Of course we are. We are!"

"Then. Isn't it ironic? I am younger but better than you were at this age. So I'm closer. If she were alive today."

Zionée was becoming furious.

"Edin, I'm real proud of you for being able to speak again. But stop it."

"She would be disappointed in you."

He pointed at the paper duck again.

"Stop it!!"

Her voice reverberated through the empty classroom. She clutched the nearest desk to prevent her shaking hand from clenching into a fist. Never had such a feeling of fierce hate possessed what was between them.

"And she would be proud," he continued, "Of me."

Suddenly Zionée remembered she was standing in front of a window and that there was still just enough light left to catch their selves in it.

"You know what? Let's have a staring contest."

Edin sat down across from her and accepted. They raced the light in their eyes to surpass the feeling that made being orphans so ominously uncertain. When her green eyes squinted she looked so much like Tessa, he couldn't believe it. Eventually, Edin squinted too dangerously close that he blinked and squeezed his eyes shut as though wincing from pain. He opened them again, facing his see-through reflection in the window. Upon seeing the way his eyes were slanted horizontally and that her nose was more Dutch than his, he could convince himself of it no more.

Accepting his defeat in his blinking, Zionée slowly smiled and got up. She walked out the door, leaving him to continue staring at his own reflection, riddled with the betrayal of golden lights that the sinking, orange glow was collecting through the glass.

9 – The Crest Riders

Zionée continued to dream of that mysterious figure silhouetted in the first light to meet her eyes. The possibility to color in those details and to illuminate those unseen features was suddenly fathomable. But no matter how hard she studied, how many records she broke, Tessa was always one step ahead of her. In the growing library of gossip her classmates were building, she would soon be a year too old for track captain championships, which Tessa had done as a sophomore. She was already too old for the freshman valedictorian record, the spot she lost the previous year to the student body president's sister due to not having taken the one, rare Advanced Placement course. Why she still believed that she could start and sustain the amount of clubs that Tessa did was an increasingly miserable mystery. She rubbed the edges of her darkening eyes, worn from circadian tears. The window was wet with condensation so she wiped it clear with her sleeve.

Her phone was quiet. Vicky still had not replied to her message of apology. Zionée quickly pocketed her phone in her skirt as the shadow of someone passed over and the hair on the back of her neck rose up like antennae. Professor Nairs's wrath was infamous when it came to cell phones. The person walked past her line of sight and she sighed with relief. It was only her classmate Pierro, who was particularly tall and heavy set. She turned her attention back to her history book on a page full of stains forensic of aged, dry coffee.

"Rigley, wake up," said Professor Nairs with a pinch of frustration in her voice. He shook wet drops of rain out of his hair in his stir and they flecked onto Zionée's hand. She feels each cold drop sink into her pores but doesn't bother to wipe it.

"Is it possible that you actually look… distracted?" Professor Nairs asked her suddenly.

"Yes, the civil rights movement did have international parallels, including regions of Africa under the brunt of apartheid."

"I asked the question for that like fifteen minutes ago," Nairs said.

"I thought I answered, Nairs. One of us must have déjà vu."

"Very funny," she said tersely.

The little tornado of chatter moved away from her and when she turned back to the window, it was already fogged up again and she could only make out a blur. A few seats away, Debby took out a sandwich in class and started sneaking bites from it whilst sharing it with Cory and Rickward. Her whispers were unusually loud.

"You guys like it? My *mother* made two more… in fact, during parent conference, my *mother* discussed how…"

Zionée blinked to control the pulse racing through her nerves at the sound of her voice. She focused her gaze on the window with the intensity of a laser beam but she turned a little so that the angle of adjust would suffice Debby, in the hopes that she would feel something hot and angry burn her. Then she tried looking to Nairs's sarcastic scuffle with Letitia and Eslamida on the world politics of NATO. Out of the corner of her eye, she could see Debby throwing a quick look at her every time she injected the word "mother" into her sentences.

"Do you have to eat every class before lunch?"

Cory and Rickward grinned at Rigley while chewing obnoxiously. Debby merely rolled her eyes.

"Didn't your mommy pack your lunch today?" she asked before squeezing her nose.

"Yes, she did. Care to try some?"

"I'll pass, thanks."

"Right, because we don't stuff ourselves in class," Rigley spoke fast. "Oh, but wait. What if I asked you outside of it?"

"Like I said, I'll pass."

"Not good enough for you?"

"No, I just have different tastes than you."

"Refined?"

"Sophisticated!"

"Oh, really like how?"

"A lot more than you!"

"Don't choke on your food now."

Debby realized she had been talking so fast that she had forgot to chew and realized what he was trying to do. She swallowed her bite and took a drink from her water while glaring at him.

"Nice try, asshole," she said, indignant.

Rigley shrugged and they all turned their attention back to the class. Zionée wiped the condensation from where his reflection was. As she moved the back of her hand slowly, mopping clear of the glass until she collected enough water to drool down her wrists, she started to see his wet reflection become clear. She wasn't sure if it was Rigley or the sensation on the back of her hand. After class was over, she packed her things in a rush and left without saying a word.

The skies were blue and full of soggy clouds. Zionée was a layer away from adapting to the cooling temperatures so she decided to stay indoors. It looked much brighter on the inside of the main building. The halls were flaring with the highly lit glow of a hospital. She couldn't bring herself to eat her lunch so she pulled her leg up against the wall, bringing her ankle close enough to her hand where she could open the little pencil case strapped to it containing a back-up reservoir of Pocky. Although the hallway was crowded with voices, some of them containing the most up-to-date rumors on Tessa, she could still hear the tiny, chocolate-coated breadstick snap between her teeth. As she leaned against the trophy cabinet, she felt back to back with Tessa. She was on the other side, like the medals and awards. Zionée knew that she had the key. Although, as she chewed the rest of the Pocky in her mouth, she was aware now that perhaps Edin had it too.

She tried to imagine what it felt like in the smaller shoe size of her brother. If Tessa were a man and looked exactly like he did, what would be going through her head? No, she revolted at the thought and limited her creativity from developing on it. It would mean surrendering to the grief that Tessa was not her mother and that she had to go back to lying to herself with all that viciously bitter strength it took to sustain her through the illusion of perfection. Back to when it was every day that she had to cling on to that singular comfort of superiority. She would hear them talking about their parents with sweet disdain and all of the love-destructive conflicts and envied even that. To have just that would have made her feel like the rest of them. She would want to be their friends.

She turned her head and looked at some students down the hall talking enthusiastically in front of the digital scoreboard. What was there for her to prove other than her own strength? Of having to renew their status as orphans every time their foster families tried to pit her against Edin? But now, against the loneliness, against the knowledge that this person's existence is as real as her own, she had something to put her conviction to the test. No more did she fear living up to this ghost, for through her, it became less of one. Where as most people needed a photograph to nurse the homesick heart, she only needed a mirror.

But Edin was the one who needed the photo.

"AP's are coming up," Flores said. Her office was a collecting mountain range of office documents and district papers. "You didn't have to call in sick to see me. That's usually something –"

"You do with your parents," Zionée finished, with her eyes half closed for a moment.

"So what's up?" Flores asked with an air of stress.

"How is my brother doing?"

Flores put her papers down for a moment.

"Edin? He's great. He's participating in class. His teachers can actually hear him now. I figured now that he's speaking—"

"Isn't it wonderful?"

"Yeah," Flores agreed. "But tell me about that enthusiasm."

Flores turned her head a little sideways and examined her forehead, a habit of her nursing school training kicking in. Zionée bit the bottom of her lip to hold her words back. She looked at her phone. Without Vicky's acceptance of her apology, she couldn't help realizing how hypocritical it was to come to Flores, who, though older, was no closer by any socially conventional means. But she was closer, Zionée thought.

"Okay," Flores pressed on. "What's going on?"

"It's nothing, I... we..."

The office phone rang and Flores answered it. She nodded to what was said to her on the receiver while Zionée watched her. There was a little desperation in her look, waiting for Flores to catch the light sparkle in her eyes but when she did not, she blinked quickly to dry them. The principal hung up and sighed, shaking her head with the weariness of someone much older, "It's the superintendant, I'm sorry. I have to go see her. And you. Oh – you!"

She checked her watch with alarm and got up in frenzy.

"You need to go back to class!"

"What does Abrams want?" Zionée asked. Superintendant Debra Abrams was Debby's grandmother. Students learned from the seniors and juniors that she was not very well liked for her strictness. Principal Flores shook her head with her eyes closed, putting one hand to her eyebrows.

"I don't know... something about reconstructing a statue."

"That old beaten up blob out there?"

"Yeah, that one."

"Our athletics department can't even pay for our own jerseys without having us sell candy."

"I hear you."

They both peered out for a moment through her blinds to see the back of the very statue in question. It was supposed to be a man but the proportions diminished it to the size of the average height of a sophomore. The gray-bronze flesh was weathered and scarred. Flores closed the blinds, flapping the blades shut with such a speed that she caused a small flutter of dust to fly at Zionee's eyes, making her flinch and wince.

"Oh shoot, sorry! Haha, are you all right?"

She nodded.

"Hey, listen you have to go to class. Every minute lost from one of Weavins's wonderful chemistry lectures is a minute you can't get back."

"Flores," she began, wiping her eye. "If there's a chance. I mean I know this is just my paranoia."

Flores stared at the name of the superintendant on the crinkled corner of an old bulletin.

"Bullies with family, huh? Scared of the acorn's distance from the tree?"

"You think Debby is a bully too?"

"I mean I can't say it. But anybody who's scared of the failure they see themselves in others can become one. It's pretty obvious she made her choice ever since you started having class together. But what do you want me to do? Put her on the spot?"

"You know what I'm talking about then."

"That Abrams will make the statue look like Tessa?"

"If you had to, could you stand up to her and say no? Flores, can you promise me? Not as a principal or a teacher. I mean as a friend."

Flores looked into her eyes absorbing as much strength from them as she could know to hold dear in herself. These were her students after all and she had to risk herself for them no matter what. She took her pencil and used the eraser tip to scratch the edge of her nose.

"Isn't that the thing you do when you make a promise to yourself?"

Zionée beamed gratefully before grabbing her one of her level 4 chemical passes and leaving out the door.

As she was going back to class, she ran into Rigley, who threw her a bag of pop tarts and was heading the opposite way. He appeared a little flustered, enough so that he couldn't stay still. She had to keep moving closer to him as he hardly stopped walking to keep their conversation within hearing distance.

"Where are you going? Why are you giving me your pop tarts?"

"Principal's office!"

Zionée gasped when she realized a black eye was growing on his face.

"Is that a black eye?!"

"It was Rickward! Don't worry, I sent myself out on a count of his self-defense. It was self-defense, because come on. Ouch, it hurts to wink."

"Self-defense?"

Rigley turned around one more time, walking backwards, and smiled. Zionée walked toward him a little to catch what he shouted.

"Yeah, the whole thing was stupid. Debby made another crack about mothers – then she brought up the state of yours – then I called her a mother-related word myself," he said before pointing to his black eye, "and guess who came to her rescue?"

"I never asked you to come to mine!" Zionée shouted. "Are you stupid?"

She clutched her sleeves and bit her lower lip, not able to think of anything else to say.

"Eat my pop tarts!" he called after her with his back turned.

When she got back to class, Debby's eyes were a little red but Rickward and Cory were still cooling off steam. Although there wasn't a single bruise on Rickward, his face was contorted with an ugly expression, warped by humiliation and indignation. She sat down next to Edmondo and Hashim and asked them what happened. Letitia put down her fashion magazine and listened in as well. They told her everything that brought her up to date with what Rigley had said and then began at another point he didn't mention.

"Yeah, then Rickward was all like 'yeah you're never going to top us in the rankings' and then me and Hashim was all like – 'what, we're not worth a spot on your radar?'"

"And then?"

"And he ignored us like all cool people do when they think they have something important to say."

"I don't ignore people when I have important things to say," said Hashim.

"Nice one," Edmondo chuckled.

Hashim stared at him indignantly for such an awkward beat as he slowly stopped laughing.

"You serious?"

"Tell her about the crest thing," Letitia said to break the tension.

"I thought he was talking about surfing," said Hashim.

Zionée threw continued glances at the back of the class to make sure that Professor Weavins was still tending to Debby and talking it out with Rickward.

"Me too," Edmondo added. "Like he's all 'yeah, at least I ride these waves better than you all and know what I want to do' something like that."

"I didn't know he could surf."

"Can you imagine Rigley surfing?"

They chuckled and continued off into more humorous tangents about surfing. Zionée slowly drifted away from it as she scratched the tip of her nose with her pencil eraser. After class, she got a text message from Edin asking to meet her at the science building's first floor. They started walking around the cafeteria and towards the courtyard in front of the main building.

"Hey," he finally said.

Zionée took out the pop tarts and shared the other one with Edin.

"You heard about Rigley?"

He nodded and took a bite.

"I thought you've really found your gift of gab."

"It's still a work in progress," Edin said, just loud enough for her to hear. Zionée looked at the statue as the caution lines were being placed around it. The renovations were about to start.

"So are Team Alpha's asses," she said.

"Then we better find a way to kick'em hard," Edin agreed.

Zionée smiled.

"That's more like it."

In the detention room, Rigley was flipping a coin sideways on the table to see how many times it could do a spherical little dance. When he heard the door open, he looked up and saw Edin and Zionée come in. The hour hand of the clock finished its revolution and it was now four in the afternoon.

"We're breaking you out," said Zionée.

"Just finished for today."

"No, for good. We're breaking you out and I will hold true to that. I will argue this with Flores until she minimizes the damage down to just a note for your parents to sign."

"You'd put your friendship on the line with the most powerful person in this school for me?"

Zionée and Edin exchanged a knowing look.

"Why not? You did. And I've made," Zionée said as she took out a small, square fold of paper with an Anime drawing on it, "A back-up note to say sorry if I end up needing to."

"That is good," Edin said. Rigley laughed to himself at how much louder he could hear him.

"I learn from the best," Zionée replied, looking at Rigley. "Come on, we've got some studying to do!"

As they walked out on campus together, gathering momentum in their pace, they smiled. They walked past the statue again, overhearing a few construction workers talk about surviving a scorpion sting. Rigley looked at Edin and Zionée.

"And Tessa?"

Zionée looked onwards. Edin watched her, anxious for her response.

"...Is a thing of yesterday. Real. Unreal. Fiction. Or Non-fiction. It doesn't matter. I'm done time traveling. I've decided to only look forward from now on. Because today I have my little brother and my best friend."

Rigley grinned but for a shadow of a second, Edin mistook it for a look of amused mischief.

"What about you Edin?"

"Yeah. I think for all we have right now. It's a pretty good thing to go on," he smiled before asking. "But what about tomorrow?"

Rigley and Zionée exchanged looks, remembering the responsibilities of catching up and getting a little further ahead in their math, science, and language classes.

"Come on," said Zionée. "Let's get to it." She had forgotten that she wanted to ask Rigley about what he really said in class.

In the next few weeks, Zionée, Rigley, and Edin studied relentlessly to close the gap between their team's GPA and that of Team Alpha's. It didn't matter that they knew Cory was inclined to cheat on tests or that Rickward and Debby were top students. It didn't faze them that they had chosen to work harder than their rivals to get sometimes lesser or equal results. Their morale and faith in each other had never been stronger. However, the other teams had also overcome their sense of interior conflict and began focusing their competitiveness outwardly. Everything that the PTA meetings have accused Flores of failing with this program was finally being proven wrong by the surprising arrival of the results she had strived to achieve. As she walked down the halls of the private sectors, visiting students individually to advise what classes they wanted to take next semester, she noticed that they all sat in the right clusters without needing the assigned seating arrangements anymore.

She eventually made it to the library where Professor Esparanza's class was being held temporarily while her room was being inspected for insects because of all the food she let her students eat. Esparanza made a small scoff of shame when she arrived, avoiding her look and focusing her attention on helping Eslamida with her "er" verbs. Flores smiled. After finishing talking to Hashim, Edmondo, and Zera about their improvement, Flores walked over to Edin's table. Zionée and Rigley came in and sat down beside him.

"You have no idea how schizophrenic this job can get," Flores said as she clicked open her pen.

They exchanged looks of bemusement. She handed them their course options.

"It's like being principal of two schools. In one class I'm keeping two kids tearing each other apart and then in the next I'm casually discussing that terrible B+ on an otherwise straight-A report card."

Zionée looked at Rigley. Flores followed her gaze to him. He checked a few courses off with his pencil and then erased it with an idle sense of indecisiveness.

"What's up, Rigs?" Flores asked.

"It's not that simple though, right? I have public friends. Some of them work harder than some people I know here. I mean just because we have…"

"Better books, teachers, and furniture?" Flores finished. She shuffled her papers and then put her hands over them before looking at them all with a scrutinizing squint. "Exactly."

Zionée chuckled and rolled her eyes. Edin just looked down at his nails. Flores raised her eyebrow at the two of them.

"Sorry, it's nothing," Zionée began. "Don't bring up publics vs. privates with this dork."

"I'm not a dork," Rigley said defensively.

"He thinks he's Tessa Seredin."

"And you don't anymore?" Flores asked. Zionée's smile faded a little. Edin shook his head as if answering for her. The principal turned to him next.

"That's awesome. Don't let your past alone decide who you are. But as we're on the topic, what have each of you decided for yourselves come tomorrow? Come a lot of tomorrows actually."

Edin tried to give an answer but held it back. Zionée watched him as if egging him on to say it. Flores started making a small crumpled ball of paper while they thought about how to answer.

"I'd like to teach, maybe," replied Edin.

Zionée looked at him, surprised.

"Really? A lot of perks to teaching," smiled Flores.

"Such as what?" asked Zionée.

"Can I borrow that slingshot I once confiscated from you, Rigley?"

"Sure."

He awkwardly took it out for her. Flores put the crumpled ball between the rubber slings and aimed it at Professor Esparanza's back. She only needed to look at Rigley to allow her inner child to let go. The ball shot into their professor's back and she turned. Students around them laughed.

"Okay! Not cool!"

Flores put the slingshot down between the three of them.

"Whichever one of you decides first and wants to tell me about it, you can take the credit."

Flores collected their course sheets, smirking at their awestruck faces. As soon as she had left the classroom, Rigley reached for the slingshot and so did Edin but it was Zionée's hand that beat them to it, surprising them both. She smiled, turning back to face Esparanza.

"Zionée! Cual es tu problema? Porque hiciste eso?"

"Lo siento, Profesora," she replied. "Yo necesito ser malo."

"Necesito ser malo?" Rigley repeated as they went to get something from their lockers before the start of their next class. "So you know what you're going to do?"

The bright, white daylight flushed out the color at the end of the hallway. Zionée stopped and didn't look at him but straight ahead when she spoke.

"No. But you do."

"Me?"

She turned to him and nodded. When they got to his locker, she opened it for him, remembering his combination after he traded it with her. "You ever see that really smart girl, sitting in the corner, chatting with friends, talking with teachers and think, 'wow, she must know.' She must know."

"Does she?"

Zionée opened her mouth and then stared at him without saying anything for a while.

"I don't know what I'm doing, Rigley, I just act like it really well. I work really hard to... act. To act like it."

She opened the locker lid all the way and gestured. Inside, behind all the AP practice books were moth-eaten volumes of Manga and little pop-up stickers of Anime characters. She took one book of the distinctly styled comics out.

"But look at you."

She pointed at his open backpack, which he had opened to take out a bottle of water. He followed her gaze to his multiple art supplies such as pen, paper, and ink.

"You really got it. The ingredients to figure out that you're in love," she stopped awkwardly.

"I'm not dead-set."

"Yes, you are. You say that, but you'd die without doing what you want to do most. And I tried to kill you over and over again."

Rigley scoffed.

"So... when did you start letting me?"

"I thought we all want that scholarship, don't we?"

"Yes, but you're not suddenly trying to –"

"Trying to what?"

"I'm just saying like – if you were doing it because of – then you've got it all mixed up."

"What have I got mixed up?"

She moved her eyes from his homework folder to his drawing book.

"What impresses me about you."

She quickly pulled out his sociology book to jump subjects before he could dwell on what she had just said, flipping through it as quickly as she could.

"And sociology. You actually know you want to help people. And that's more than getting good grades and being the best at everything could ever say about me."

"You don't have to be in a hurry to figure it out," Rigley said.

The light from the sky outside got a lot dimmer but the hallway remained luminous from the glare of ceiling lamps. They felt safer because of it.

"Oh yeah? All the tests, SATs, AP exams, college credit classes, sports meets, community service, all of it tells me differently. Everybody, my teachers, my foster parents, my coaches, my classmates... everybody except..."

Rigley raised his eyebrows comically to ask her who the exception was. She took out a small model kit of a robot that she was building and put on the last piece. It had colors of blue, yellow, and white.

"I used to follow the booklet instructions. But now I rebuild it a different way. It helps me figure out how differently you must think. I don't know why I started to care but –"

He laughed and sat down beside her after she closed her locker.

"This chapter is a flashback," she said, opening her Manga and flipping it to the page that she had bookmarked. "They do that a lot of that while fighting."

As Rigley looked over at it, his eyes lit up with an energy that Zionée hungered for. "I haven't read this week's yet. Is this one from the new –"

"What did you say to Rickward and Debby before you got sent out of class last week?" she interrupted. "I heard from Edmondo and Hashim that it was something about crests and waves but I know it wasn't about surfing –"

Rigley put down the Manga but didn't remove his hand from the page.

"Oh that. Ha, so I was getting pretty mad. They were taking the piss out of me for being an underachiever. Saying that I'd never get a high-paying job because I'd mess up too much with the calculations. I told them that I might mess up my calculations in here…"

He pointed to his head and Zionée lowered her eyes until her pupils were enclosed with a lazy look of familiarity. Then she pointed at her chest and smiled.

"But at least you don't in here?"

"Am I really that?"

Rigley's eyebrows rose up in a frown, self-conscious. Zionée smiled and laughed, finding this revelation that he could be vulnerable in that way too to be comforting.

"A bit. I kid. Go on."

He looked at her and smiled slowly as he spoke.

"I said that I am going to be the greatest…"

Rigley dropped his head down with sarcastic despair as Zionée laughed before he could finish because of how much he reminded her of one of her Anime characters.

"What do you think then? Without knowing what I think of you?"

Zionée stopped and looked up at the glass pane above them, too high up from their angle to see themselves in. There was more color in her face than she had ever recognized herself to have.

"So… what do you?"

"I absolutely despise you," he said cheekily.

Zionée squinted at him and smiled. They were both silent. He continued looking off into space, at their faint silhouetted reflections in the white, metal lockers. He started to speak again and this time from a dark and distant place. His voice sounded lower and older than it had ever did before. Zionée clenched her fingers into a fist, slightly grazing her knuckles against the cold floor.

"What I said was this. All our lives we've been taught to ride the waves of other people's expectations. Other people's dreams. After a while the crest builds and builds and you lose footing on your own. And then you lose track of how many times you have to pinch yourself to wake up from the one that isn't yours."

They pinched each other and closed their eyes as though praying. Then Rigley bolted up to Zionée's surprise. He helped her up to talk to her on the level.

"I'm my own crest rider. I may ride the expectations of others. But I never forget my own. Because I know whatever I'm going to fall in love with doing in this life, I'm going to be greatest at it! That's how I'll know the dream is mine."

Zionée's eyes appeared to change to a brighter color from his reflection lighting up in them as he moved closer. She started tapping her fingers rhythmically out of nervousness until suddenly, what all those years of purging her feelings have made her forgot unwound like a bolt from the deepest vault of her mind.

"I think I... know!! I think I know now!"

She blinked decisively and slowly.

"What? Really? You know your crest?"

She took out a taped-up, old Japanese Character CD album and showed it to him. "I want to sing and rock out in a Japanese pop band! And write songs for my favorite Anime characters! And..."

She suddenly pulled him into a pace after kicking the locker behind them. They ran down the stairs excitedly shouting, building off of the knowledge of each other.

"Play the bass! And sing completely in Japanese! Edin and me took some music lessons when we were kids!"

"This is awesome! You can totally go for it!"

Rigley leapt to the bottom of the steps before Zionée so she jumped on the rail and slid the rest of the way down, catching his hand in a clasp and spun a hug around him with such awkwardness and force that they both crashed to the floor. She laughed, getting up from atop of him and helping him up.

"That's my crest! I'm not going to forget it! Because it makes me want to be who I am! Happy with who I am! I can't wait for it all! The low self-esteem! Hating myself for even trying! Thinking I'll never succeed and get any better! Get depressed by how much my talent sucks compared to others!"

"And then from there you'll improve, right?"

They ran past classrooms with their loud chatter and made such a ruckus that teachers and students were beginning to stick their heads out.

"No! First I'm going to remember how I met this underachiever boy in high school who's grades were really abysmal at first and he like sucked at doing everything!"

As they left the main building and took a turn between the auditorium and the science building, they headed down towards the history building and then turned again. They both leapt onto a trolley that was used for moving crates and kicked it off, sliding fast down the slope. As they approached the bungalows at the bottom of it, they jumped off and rolled, getting a few bloody scabs but laughing nonetheless.

"Man, that really fucking hurt," winced Zionée.

"Yeah, let's not do that again," Rigley added.

Despite the pain singing from their knees and their elbows, they started running behind the bungalows before the janitors could see them.

"And then I'll think about how he got – against all odds – better. And better. Until he got to where he is today. And then I'll think about where he's going tomorrow."

Rigley stopped panting in time to laugh.

"And then I'll know who to follow it into. And from there… I'll never give up! Because I'll be the best at what I do too! And that's how I will know the dream is mine!"

They were almost to Professor Xen's room in the bungalows. The sky was a dark, blue-gray shade of night. But a towering spiral of fire was circling fast within them both like a brightly burning torch newly alighted by their reincarnated meeting. Zionée stepped on Rigley's foot by accident as they made it up the small steps leading to the math classrooms. She didn't skip any this time. Before they went through the door, they stopped, catching their breaths.

"I think I will believe in you, Zionée Dunnelin," said Rigley.

"I think I will believe in you, Rigley Kurosawa," Zionée laughed, filled with bubbling happiness and a newfound determination. The air was cold with the smell of rain and wet pavement.

10 – Fire Alarms

The statue continued to gradually sculpt itself into a recognizably human shape in the stressful weeks leading up to the AP exams. The bronze hue was slowly being painted over with iridescent shades of ghostly grays. Its once smooth slate of a face now had pronounced eyes, a mouth, and even a haircut. In the middle of a patch of grass in the exterior corner of the main building, it stood on a pedestal surrounded by yellow ribbons. Edin noticed Edmondo and Hashim hanging out near the staircase leading to the first entrance of the west wing. He walked up to them and dropped his backpack down. They nodded up at him. He didn't remove his gaze from the distant stone figure, looking pale and eerie from the few yards away it stood. When enough people crowded around that corner of the courtyard, it could almost be camouflaged as one of them.

"I think it has eyes now," said Edmondo. "It didn't have eyes yesterday."

"No," agreed Hashim. "Definitely not."

"How's your Team doing?" Edin asked.

"Actually if you noticed we've recently caught up to number three," Hashim said.

"Yeah, don't worry Edin, we're not going to beat your team. You have Zionée on it. And Rigley doesn't suck so much anymore."

Edin took out a pencil case and offered them some Pocky.

"Don't be so hard on yourselves," he told them, holding out the chocolate-coated sticks of cookie. Edin showed them how to eat it like edible cigarettes.

"Thanks. Anyways, we don't even care if Team Alpha-douches win," Edmondo said.

Edin's eyebrows furrowed.

"Why?"

"APs. Far more important than some Team Ranking program title. Some of us have different AP classes and are taking different exams. Priorities, you know? Plus if we won, it'd just be one more reason for the publics to hate us."

Edin furrowed his eyebrows and looked at him peculiarly.

"You didn't know, Edin?" Hashim began. "The scholarship money for the team that wins is taken directly from the school budget arranged for the publics."

"Why would Flores do something like that?"

"I don't think that she would," said Edmondo.

"Abrams," agreed Hashim.

"Either way, you can't just give up," Edin said.

They looked at him, bemused.

"Sometimes it's more important to try to win than it is to."

"Man, ever since you've been hanging out with Rigley, you say cheesy stuff like that."

"You can ignore me."

"Sure," Edmondo said. "But this time, I won't."

"Neither will I," added Hashim.

Edin had forgotten that all this year they weren't just studying for high school credit but in a good many tomorrows they would need credit for college. Rigley took AP English and AP European History. Zionée took both of these along with AP Chemistry and AP Physics. They went to the student shop last Thursday to order their exams and were able to get discounts because their foster parents had recently declared bankruptcy. It was a shift in their financial background that they were prepared to take advantage of despite how they still made their own lunches. Some construction workers showed up around the statue and began making plans with the architect. They took out a blueprint and gestured a lot as though they were planning to build something on a much larger scale than a human-sized monument. Zera arrived, popping out of the front entrance doorway with her breath short from running. She was already in her blue track jersey.

"Hey guys, I just wanted to tell you that I won't be able to go to the Chem study session because I'm taking an AP Bio practice exam today."

"Okay, good luck."

Zera raised her eyebrows at them and nodded.

"So, it's okay then?"

"Yeah," Edmondo repeated, a little annoyed.

"Yeah, okay. Good luck on your exams too."

After all the time she spent studying with them in the library, Zera had been working hard to fix her schedule and within a couple of weeks, her grades were improved. Subsequently, Team Beta's ranking had benefited in rising up to third place, right below Omega.

"Hey Edin. I haven't heard you speak yet. Is it true?"

Edin hesitated.

"Hi."

"That's so cool. Awesome."

Zera ignored the continuity of enmity that Edin brought into his monotone response. She turned to the statue. "You guys know what I heard about that statue?"

They all turned towards it. The construction workers left for their lunch break but their bright, yellow construction helmets rested on the ground like large, awkward seashells. Edin's ears piqued with interest.

"Supposedly. It's going to be a monument for this student who changed the school."

Edin's ears perked up at this but Zera shook her head at him.

"I doubt it. She wasn't just an overachiever, Edin. Trust me, I know my rumors when I say that Tessa Seredin was definitely the sort who was always popular."

"What does that have to do with anything?"

"Can you imagine someone who was ever lonely enough to be bothered by this kind of thing to want to change it all?"

Edin did not remove his gaze from the statue nor did he let go of what his feelings projected.

"Good point," said Hashim. "I mean there are always those extreme social worker kids but it's definitely not something worth sacrificing being a teenager over. I hear even Flores toned down all her integration talk just because the other teachers made fun of her."

"Right? See?" she nodded. "My theory makes sense."

Zera sneezed into her hand before wiping it on the stone rail. Edmondo removed his hand from the rail with disgust.

"Anyways, Hashim, we have to go to Track. Coach wants to see us about the upcoming meet."

He grabbed his things and exchanged goodbyes with Edin and Edmondo.

"I'll say hi to your sister for you!" Zera called after Edin. They ran off toward the track field on the other side of campus.

"You know you should try out for a sport too," Edmondo told him.

Edin shrugged and began speaking softly.

"I had a dream I played baseball in a major league stadium. I was better in-field and I didn't strike out the first time like I thought I would. It didn't go far but I hit it, so I was able to run to second base before they retrieved it. Then I just stayed there."

"Don't stay, man," Edmondo chuckled. "Keep going."

"So are you cool with Zera, now?"

"What with all the time she's taking away from Hashim?"

"No, I mean from all the time she's finally putting into the team."

Edmondo's face blushed and he looked to the side.

"Oh yeah, man. Yeah. That's what I thought you meant."

After school, Edin walked across the grassy mound where all of the snobs parked their posses at during lunch and found its vacant emptiness to be fulfilling. He detested how something so invisible, so intangible, and so insignificant as the order of the people they spent their lives with could dictate where people hung out and whom they hung out with. Ever since he and his sister stopped suppressing their emotions with their ritual, he could see through layers of facades. An impulse arose as he took a deep breath. He was sometimes angry enough to tear the whole place up and destroy this little paradise that they barred from the world. Recalling how Zera had been nice to them this afternoon, Edin's indignation felt warped. Whenever one of these snobs did something noble, it would seem to usurp all of their past vileness. It was how everyone got by casually on the fact that they were left stranded on the beach and the only people properly punished were strange fill-ins whom posed under their names and weren't even from this school.

As Edin tore out the grass beside him until he got to the roots that connected clumps of dirt together, he could hear someone coughing. He listened more carefully. The voice was feminine and whimpering. She was on the phone and he started to move his things but stopped. It was late and they were the only two left out on the grass mound. He became very conscious of her and didn't want to seem rude. She had pretty, brown hair and lots of freckles.

"Oh, hey dad," she said to her phone. The innocent sound of her voice made the savage vengeance weaken inside of him. She was on the phone with her father. "No, I'm not crying. It's my science teacher. He's such an asshole!"

She sniffed her nose and she wiped her eyes with her sleeves. Edin knew that she meant Professor Weavins.

"Sorry I didn't mean to cuss, but I need you to hear me out."

She breathed between her own gasp of surprise and a small wave of relief as though saying it had suddenly made her feel better.

"What did he say to me? With a batting average like mine, I should just stick to softball and focus more on my grades. I love baseball. But dad. Hey, no, you're supposed to be on my side! Dad! No! I'll bring my grades up just don't make me! You can't take his side! I am so getting better! No, why don't you just say it then? I should quit! I hate you!"

She clapped her flip phone loudly and suppressed her angry cries in her arms, which she folded over her knees. Then she threw the phone into her backpack with a needless intensity. Edin watched as her silhouette became silent. When she lifted her head again, he could see the orange, sunset light shining wetly on her face. Suddenly her eyes moved to him, catching him noticing her. Edin quickly turned away but when he turned back, he noticed she was still looking at him. After drying her eyes, she got up.

There was a baseball mitt strapped to her backpack bobbing against it as she walked out of there. When she got to the trashcan by the edge of the fence, she tore it off the string with a grimace and chucked it in. The last curtain drapes of daylight retracted into the horizon.

Edin and his sister had almost every kind of foster parent, whom out of the kindness in their hearts, put roofs over their heads. But the houses were not insulated with love so much as material curiosity. Somehow, back in a time when he was still unlearning his ability to speak, they had adults posing as parents in a way that scarred their trust for all fosters from then on. They couldn't help but be cold and untrusting. The only ones they had to suffer it all through were each other. They had rotated around so many different classes and people by now, they lost track of the memories of when each did what. Consequently, they also lost all sense of status and so they had to make their own. When they got home, their fosters watched them curiously as they haunted the building like a reminder of some newly purchased decoration that they didn't know what to do with. What they all had in common was the tendency to pit Zionée against him, and he, against her. Whenever it happened, the enmity would begin and they would go online and search for new adoptees.

In the beginning, none of Edin's talents or achievements could persuade anyone to adopt him but Zionée always forcefully insisted that she couldn't be adopted without him. He had her to thank for keeping the very ground where he stood under his feet. This love, something he was once very grateful for, now had him boiling with an irreconcilable and mysterious rage. He took out Rigley's sketchbook and flipped through countless pages of his attempts at Anime drawings. There was a little, red see-through flag that bookmarked where Zionée's drawings began. Page after page, he noticed her improvement in comparison to his was jarring and dramatic. The lines and proportions all found reason and shape faster than his. He continued flipping through it until he accidentally came upon the sepia leaf that reflected back in time. Slowly, he lifted the newspaper cutout of Tessa Seredin and stared as the details became too hard to discern in the growing darkness.

The metallic cacophony continues on like a bad migraine in Yogun's head. He removes his green bandana from his ears and sighs before walking down the hall where Tessa is punching the lockers in the last isle. Today is the day of the annual summit meeting between the major gangs of the school's public sector.

"You know they did invent the punching bag," he says.

Tessa closes her sleepless eyes.

"Is Janet still dating that –?" she asks and obscures the last foul word with a loud slam of the locker and then throws another double round of knuckled applause.

"Yep."

"Good then at least I've got nothing left to lose."

"She's your friend again."

Tessa makes a frustrated noise out of her mouth and then nods like she is prepared to fight an army.

"Hey. You've been acting a little tense."

"Oh just a little," they hear Alonzo say in the background.

"Look man," Yogun continues, "Calm down and stop preparing for this like you're going into a boxing match. This is diplomacy."

"Exactly!"

Yogun rubs his eyebrows as she continues to punch the metal lockers with greater force and speed. His tone changes and he takes off his reading glasses.

"Hey! Listen to me. What have you learned? Huh, Tesla?"

Tessa stops punching the lockers and becomes still. She doesn't speak for a moment, realizing herself. Her knuckles pulsate as she recollects herself.

"Thanks. For calling me that."

"You're welcome. Whether you hate or like or come to understand people, no matter how different they are from you, the literacy of the streets I've been teaching you are about looking past what comes easiest to the eyes. And here, that means that we're not all about being thugs."

Tessa calms down, realizing how quickly her bias protected her when she is the most afraid and shakes her head, finding herself despicable.

"I'm sorry."

"Ah, it's cool. I know we all forget that sometimes, especially us publics. Good to know you're one of us. All right? It's okay, man. You're one of us."

"Takes a hell of a lot to convince though," says Alonzo moodily. Tessa looks off to the side like she feels ashamed of something.

"Alonzo. You're not helping. And you, loosen your hands."

With great effort, Tessa loosens her hands from the tight fist-hold she had them in. They walk out to the empty basketball courts, which make up a vacuous stage of asphalt littered with cafeteria tray remnants. It is after school and they are all out, cast under the light of a dense, gray sky.

"Sup everyone," Yogun begins. He walks into the center of the court, wrapping his bandana around his fist before holding it out. "Now, as you all know. I'm about to be graduating pretty soon. This'll probably be the last time you see me."

Yogun and Tessa look around at all of the dangerous and aggressive looking classmates whom are fully wrapped up in the armor of street literacy; full of hand-me-down clothes stained with the battles of their older brothers. They are a modestly diverse group coming from a lot of the same neighborhoods that are littered about the rims of the suburban shell surrounding the school.

"One way or another," Tessa hears Yogun nervously whisper to himself. He clears his throat and continues. "The vacuum I leave behind would, to my knowledge, leave a pretty dangerous struggle for everybody's favorite thing next to respect... called power."

One of the other gang leaders emerges forward to speak and holds up his fist with his bandana wrapped around it. He is a large, burly lumberjack gangster.

"Hold up!"

"Be my guest."

"I think whatever you're saying is real interesting and all but it's not relevant anymore. It ain't just about us now. It's everyone. It's going to be chaos. Why? Because somebody has defaced the graffiti mural. And we all know this ain't like some blog being taken down. It's our entire history."

Tessa scoffs. If chaos isn't having to decide a person's social disposition by how well they survive a brutal fight, she does not know what is. The gang leader turns to her.

"Somebody who is the real topic of today's discussion. Somebody from your gang."

"Yeah!"

The other gangs continue to shout in agreement. Finally, Tessa steps past Yogun and takes his place in the gritty arena.

"You guys want to say something to me?"

"We saying the last person we saw come out from the basement was you!"

Alonzo steps forward into the middle of the court and raises his fist with his bandana wrapped around it.

"Hold up!"

The other groups oblige him by virtue of his being friends with many of their members. He turns to Tessa and Yogun and nod at them.

"There was this kid. From one of y'all gangs. None of you, I bet, remember him but he was expelled for bringing in a street knife and a pistol. They found it in his locker. You know who it was meant for?"

They all exchange looks of excitement and paranoia. Alonzo turns to Yogun.

"That's right. It was meant for me," Yogun says. Alonzo walks around, returning the accusatory glare back at all of them.

"Now this foo' was prolly from one of your gangs. But like I said none of you would remember until you needed to. Until he became a reason to start shit up. Sometimes we are just motivated by a greed to be evil. And it's real funny for a while, isn't it? On a timeline. On a real small portion of the timeline. Until we get to a point where it's too late."

As he speaks, Alonzo still feels the tinge of betrayal from Yogun for not choosing him to be his succeeding rep. He briefly glares in Tessa's direction.

"But other times we wise up. Other times we stand up. My homeboy right here. Do you know who he is?"

Tessa's hands clench nervously. They all turn their accusatory eyes at her. A small percussion of still healing bones rattle amongst their sleeves. Tessa pulls her gloves on more tightly.

"He's the fool who stood up for the fool, who grew up at the end of the year into a thug who tried to take down my brother here."

Yogun shake his head with a mix of pride and disbelief. Alonzo nods to Tessa with respect in his eyes.

"Then he's just as much to blame," says another gang member.

"Hold up. I'm not done. You say he is to blame because you know who he was standing up for. But you don't know what he was standing up to. The boys who beat up this kid and made him dream everyday of his life of killing all of us? They are right here."

Tessa squints, suddenly understanding their gang's diplomatic strategy. She turns to Yogun, who is smiling proudly at Alonzo.

"Where are they then, huh?" challenges a gang leader.

"Right here," says a voice. To his shock, one of his own members walks forward. It is Janet's cousin.

"And right here," says another voice. His friend comes out from another opposing gang and Tessa starts to see that this whole situation is built upon a Shakespearian convenience.

"And also, right here," says Emilio.

"Can't you see that our gangs don't mean much in the way of survival anymore? Not as much as whatever it is these guys have got going. Know what that is? Guilt. That's what we got. That's what we all got. Not just us. But all y'all."

"Who are you to judge us?" another tall leader in a black bandana says as he walks forward. "I want to know who defaced the mural already!"

"Maybe you guys should stop relying on a colorful wall to tell you how to run your lives," Tessa suddenly says. They turn to her.

"Hold up," she says, quickly remembering to wrap her bandana around her fist and holding it up.

"At least it's got more color than you," a blonde, spiky-haired leader in baggy clothes says. All of the groups laugh. Tessa ignores this.

"Look at us. Any normal kind of world, we'd all be in different groups. We'd be on sports teams or part of clubs. That's what the privates have and it isn't a whole lot but it still is a privilege. Ask yourselves, then, why are we divided in gangs? Why do we have to be divided in gangs? You say it's to look cool. You say it's to represent something you believe in. To protect something. Community. You know what I believe in?"

They all shake their heads impatiently. Yogun cues Tessa to get to them fast by pointing to his wrist.

"Fire alarms. I know I may be white, but I also know what it's like to be poor. Just like how some of you aren't but know what it's like not to be. Fire alarms. Every night, they'd go off in my apartment but there never was any fire I could see or smell. Something is wrong. We're all bullied by something bigger than we can control... until the only way we feel like we're safe or strong is if we bully something smaller. Shit. Shit. Fuck. Fuck. Bitch. Bitch."

They all look at each other. Even the toughest of them begin to wince and wear from the strength of these words.

"Do you hear it? It's like a morse code. For what? We're so insecure with how scarred and ugly we've become on the inside that that's all we get used to seeing on the outside. Fire alarms. Help me turn them off. Each one of us here is in a gang because we want to forget the fear that make us need to belong to something bigger than our own individual weaknesses. And you know what that fear is? It's being too afraid to go school to and get to worry about homework like normal kids do because somebody may be busting your balls. I say forget it. Guys who bust balls to feel like they have a pair will never be real men."

Tessa stops herself for a moment to catch her breath. She blinks her eyes dry.

"The kid I stood up for at the end of the year had, I had no idea he was gonna bring a gun to school. But I would not go back in time to stop myself for even one second from letting him get humiliated if I thought that second would count because it doesn't. He would have brought that gun a lot sooner. We failed to give him one thing, it just takes one thing, to know that you deserve a little respect when everyone else has taken it away: a friend. And that's what we all should be. Not liars. Not bullies. And not gangs. We're a public school. We're better than what those who look down on us imagine us to be. How? Because we are classmates educated under the same literature of pain. And that pain smarts. That pain smarts."

They are all quiet. Their silence and attentiveness is all the applause Tessa needs. As she begins walking away, one gang member walks forward with his fist out.

"Hold up!"

She stops and turns around.

"All them pretty words ring straight with us but they also translate to all the reasons someone would need to deface the mural. Do you deny that?"

Before she can speak, Yogun walks forward.

"He doesn't have to."

He looks at them all bravely.

"All y'all got one more chance to have a go at me. I did it. However messed up your social lives get as a consequence, I'm prepared to take responsibility."

Tessa spins around but he raises his hand up to let her know it is going to be okay. Their thirty minutes are up and it is too late. "Meeting concluded," they all say. They disperse, angrier but wiser to what they are dealing with.

Alonzo and Tessa both turn to Yogun with confused looks.

"What the hell, man?!"

"Hey. Listen to me. I've been training you all year but I feel like I've come away learning more. So now I got to show you how."

"By putting yourself in danger?" Tessa asks.

"By trusting you. And you," he says, turning to Alonzo, who shakes his head with a very worrisome look. Yogun gives them both a calm look of confidence. Then he takes his bandana out of his pocket and stares at it quietly for a moment before giving it to Tessa. "Whatever happens now, my rep is yours. As soon as they make the move – you're the gang's leader."

"Are you crazy, man?" Alonzo says. "You're going to get yourself killed."

Yogun holds his disheveled, old history book up.

"Then I guess there'd be no more point in me studying for finals, huh?"

They stand there looking dumbfounded as he walks away, grabbing his backpack and getting ready to study.

"Well," Alonzo asks. "What now?"

Tessa watches Yogun move through the grimy asphalt littered with cafeteria food. A small scatter of spring leaves dance with plastic bag partners under the prom breeze of fall. The horizon is dark and dilapidated but he is walking like he can see a different one.

"We make sure he graduates and gets out of here before anybody can do anything stupid."

"What are you going to do?"

She takes a deep breath.

"I'm going to dissolve the gangs and unite the whole school."

"Fool, you're crazy."

Tessa turns towards the light in the principal's office.

"Good, cause I'll need to be if I'm going to pull it off."

11 – Secret of Time Travel

Under a stormy, gray sky Zionée walked to the statue by the corner of the main building where her brother texted to meet her. The callus was dense on her fingers, which were sore from bass lines. Her stride was listless and jumpy but she slowed to a calm when she saw him standing opposite to the statue, with his head down, and his face in shadow from the dimness of the overcast. Suddenly, he turned his head up at the statue. When she walked up to him, he didn't look away as he spoke.

"You've stopped taking your medicine."

She slowly followed his gaze up at the statue.

"Is that…?"

Edin nodded. The thought of encouraging him to follow his passions with music suddenly evaporated into smoke.

"What are they playing at?" she said with building panic. Raindrops, light and invisible, splashed into her eyes for a moment. She blinked them away as the horror became more clear.

"You don't believe she's real anymore?"

Go ahead. Tell him about the music, she thought with a mind that was starting to quake with anger that it shook all else out of balance.

"It doesn't matter if I believe it or not!! They – whoever they are – have no right to do something like this! This fucking joke has gone too far! How could Principal –?"

"Stop being so self-centered."

Zionée lost her breath. Edin was never more loud and clear. His gray-blue eyes were like cold sapphire.

"A joke? You think our mother is a joke? You think both Flores and the state district have the time to waste messing with the head of a single student? Egocentripetal motion, Zionée!"

"NO!!" she screamed. The wind turned sharp and chilly around them as raindrops began to freckle the concrete. Zionée turned but Edin grabbed her by the shoulders and turned her to face the statue again.

"Look at her!"

"Why are you doing this?"

"Look at her!"

Edin let go of her and continued shouting at her. The school grounds were empty and his voice echoed loudly. "You would have us forget our own mother just when the chance to believe we ever had one should come to light! It's come to light!"

Zionée lost control of her breathing and shook her head repeatedly. The air was growing more brisk and dense with water. Soon, the rain polished the stone ghost until it shined from its wetness. It took all her strength to deny what her own eyes were registering, the sight of which continued to choke the air out of her lungs.

"Egocentripetal motion, sis. You've had too much of it."

She stopped and looked from the statue to Edin. Suddenly he became even more frightening. His wet forehead frowned. His eyes looked sad and he spoke as though he were pleading. There were tiny droplets that collected around the tips of his eyelashes. His softer, younger voice echoed his boyish appearance.

"The school has every right to make a monument out of one student's sacrifice to make it better than what it was before."

"Sacrifice?" breathed Zionée.

He turned away from her to face the statue as he spoke.

"She should be alive; at least in her 40s. She should be famous. She should be on TV or the latest scientific journal or something. Every night, before you go to sleep, I search through every professional field. Every possible query and there is not a trace of Tessa Seredin. You know why? Our mother's dead, sis. She's dead before we ever got to meet her. Before the world did. The only world that ever knew her was this one... Sheltevue. And you know it's great that you finally figured out what you want to do."

Edin took something out of his backpack. It was a badly folded, blue origami crane representing a grade report.

"But we're not going to beat Team Alpha that way, are we?"

Zionée stood, frozen in place.

"Isn't it ironic though? How we thought Rigley would be the one to bring us down? But it's you. Look at what's happened to you."

She sunk back against the statue and closed her eyes in pain.

"It's just a B!!"

"What did she die for?"

Edin calmly waited for his sister's cry to finish echoing in the stillness.

"I don't think doing less than what she's set the bar for us to achieve is going to help us figure that out."

She looked at him desperately but angrily.

"What will, then?"

Edin nodded up in the direction of the science building and started walking towards it. Zionée grabbed her backpack and walked a few paces before stopping, feeling the statue gazing at her back. The raindrops tickled the back of her cold neck. Tempted to almost turn around, she persisted in walking forward and following her brother to the mysterious arena of his challenge.

Bolts of lightning crashed high above the skies, rumbling through the thick walls of the science room. Zionée and Edin both slapped their chemistry books down flat open on the table. They quickly flapped to the page where the marathon problem Tessa Seredin had been famous for solving was written. The massively intricate cluster of chemistry equations sprawled over two pages with soggy, wet edges. They both took out equal measures of the required chemical substances and began. Zionée wiped her forehead dry. As they started writing out the problem, Edin was keeping up with her and getting all of the initial calculations. They could still smell the scent of rain and wet soil from their shoes.

Every once and a while their eyes would meet while they turned on their rotating chairs and they'd squint spitefully at each other. The egocentripetal motions spun them up until the energy they absorbed had them boiling with a rage as extreme as the temperatures of their solvents. As soon as the little timers buzzed in sync, they began calculating the next part of the problem while simultaneously preparing for the titration. Inside them both were two little hares running across a meadow trying to catch the shadow they were divided from. Edin felt a small bump of acne forming near his temple. After the titration, they furiously punched in the keys of their Texas instruments to calculate the error ratio. As soon as their pencils stopped burning lead against paper, they dropped back to their chairs, exhausted. There, on their notebooks, was an answer. Only one of them would be a worthier solution to the question Tessa Seredin's answer posed. Their eyes moved away from the blank ceiling and met. Edin's left eye twitched a little to keep from almost faltering. After seeing the triumphant flash of confidence in them, it was Zionée's who blinked this time. He didn't care that they were the shape of Tessa's.

Edin grabbed his notebook and walked up to the table between them where the answer key was perched. Zionée watched him for his reaction. Edin turned around and grabbed his backpack. He headed out the doorway without another word. Zionée walked over to the aged chemistry book with Tessa's answer on it and then looked at her own. Her hand shook. She remembered watching their Team Ranking drop back down to three. Now, looking at the number incurred physical pain. She was just a biological coincidence. There was a swelling vacuum of terror starting to warp from inside of her as she ran after Edin upon seeing the new result. Their error ratios had almost completely switched. Edin's was now closer to Tessa's where as her own had fallen dramatically.

When she caught up to him near the entrance to the library, she pulled him around and demanded to know how he got his answer. It was dark and the only lights revealing half of their features were from the open doors of the library, leaving the rest of them in shadow.

"I didn't cheat if that's what you're thinking," Edin said calmly. "Or I wouldn't be as surprised as you are."

Zionée did her best to fight back tears. She swallowed them back with each forceful blink.

"Well, why aren't you proud?"

"Egocentripetal motion."

She stepped backwards, for the first time seeing something of the monster she created.

"It's hard, I know," Edin consoled. "But you can still be related to me. To be related to Tessa."

"How?" Zionée mouthed without any sound. Her voice was breaking from all of the pain and crushing humiliation of being outdone by somebody so much younger than her.

"If you can go back in time to who you were when you said you didn't need anyone. Would you?"

"But I was so mean to you," she mouthed again. But she nodded to make sure that he wouldn't misread her.

"Yeah. All I was to you was just your proof for how only someone related to you could surpass you. I just thought the day I did, you would be proud."

"How do I go," she gasped, "Back?"

"I have a way of doing that," Edin said, turning from the shadows again so that his face was in the light. "You're going to be fine. You'll pass all of your APs. You'll be the top of your class again. But we won't be the winning team. This is a much lonelier victory. Because that's the only kind that can restore your place beside me and Tessa again."

"How do I go back in time?" she said, this time with enough force to break above a whisper. Edin turned away. The classroom light that was illuminating the side of his face slipped off and he was enveloped in shadow. He took a deep breath.

"You have to break your best friend's heart."

Flores walked up to Zionée's classroom during period four and considered going in but decided not to. She leaned in and overheard her voice, happy and normal, participating in a comical conversation with Professor Tammy. Everything seemed all right so far. She looked up at the mirror glass panes she had proudly lobbied for to be added to the school hallways. Despite how much eyeliner she put on, she could still see the accusatory look in her eyes. A student walked by and pointed at a ticking noise coming from a locker. Flores quickly ran to the tall, lanky brown haired boy.

"What have you got in there?"

"A clock?" he said with a deadpan expression. She squinted at him disbelievingly.

"Oblige me," Flores demanded.

He opened the locker and took out a clock with a cute, animal cartoon on it. She examined the rest of its empty, metallic belly only to find a few books and magazines – nothing of alarm to confiscate.

"All right, sorry about that."

Flores walked to the end of the hallway and looked out the windowsill where the statue renovations continued to take place. The little circles of bright, yellow construction hats moved like sprites around the gray, demolition block. There didn't seem to have been any sculpting being done yet and the whole process seemed more anatomical and surgical, as though the thing was alive. A couple of birds flew past the trees surrounding the edges of the courtyard and over the metal fences where students hopped to get fast food during lunch. Flores contemplated positioning a few more security guards at that area but the fights usually broke out around the food courts.

"When are you going to stand up to her?" came an amused voice behind her. Flores turned around to be joined by Nairs.

"The superintendant?"

"Debra talks to her granddaughter. She knows Zionée is your favorite student. She has a salary that makes her think she can own us."

"I don't need a history lesson, Nairs."

Nairs sat down on the opposite edge of the windowsill cubby. She shuffled out a few bottles of soda and juice that she confiscated from her freshman and offered one to the principal. Flores took the orange juice.

"Then I assume you've already made the connections."

"Zionée's going to have to be tough about this. She has been, all year. But I won't let anything happen to her. Not to any of my students."

They were quiet all except for the sound of the soda lid being popped open.

"You should sit with us," said Nairs casually. "During lunch, at the teacher's lounge."

Flores looked at her as she finished her soda, stood up, and headed down the stairs. She was speechless and quickly rubbed her eyes a little self-consciously to remove some of the excess eyeliner.

Zionée avoided going to Flores's office for days now. Vicky's response to her apology never came. During track, Zionée tripped and fell, rolling painfully just inches away from the finishing line. The other runners ran past her. She picked herself up and limped off of the track with her sprained ankle. By the bleachers, she saw the shiny glint of their picture phones sparkling. The legions of beautiful, brainy privates whom have been nourished by her hatred in the past now reciprocated in battalions. She could feel the snobs' wrath, collecting like a distant tidal wave, vindictive in the force of its weight, as it would soon come crashing down on her.

In the locker room, Zera came in and asked if she was all right. She shook her head. She gave her an ice pack and a towel before returning to the other side of the locker to talk about the race with the rest of the track team. Zionée sat alone in the empty isle, cracking her foot back in place, with her face silently reacting to the screaming agony with the discipline of a soldier. She didn't need anybody to stand up for her. The light spilled into the over-scented, smelly chamber through the netted windows. It glowed so brightly that Zionée allowed herself for a moment to think, after the pain diminished enough for her to be able to do so, it would be a clear, beautiful sky waiting on the other side.

The sky is damp and cloudy and the wind is cold enough to cool sweat. Tessa meets with Alonzo and Janet by the dirt-covered bleachers during a soccer game. It is a typical grudge match between privates and publics but, oddly enough, this time the people sitting in the stands are actually cheering for both sides. They are losing the game but the referee does not care about the fouls going on. There are a few publics on the private team and some privates on the public team. They are quiet as the sound of distant whistles ring out below. Alonzo scoffs as he watches a goalie kick a ball off the field, fighting with the referee.

"How did they know when he was going to go to the bathroom?"

Their campaign to keep their former leader safe is threatened by the recent planting of a chemical explosive in the bathroom.

"What's important is that we knew in time to tell him not to," says Tessa bitterly. "They must have used food or something. The nurse said that he would be all right."

A silent ice cream truck drives a donut on the street past the school fences. Everyone stops playing to watch. Tessa stares past the field before turning to Alonzo.

"Does Yogun have any friends that we don't know about?"

"You mean privates? Sure. I mean I know a few myself."

Tessa looks away for a moment and watches a penalty kick.

"I meant to be more specific. Does he have any friends who look like they are privates?"

Alonzo nods. Tessa notices Janet's distinct look of someone who has just changed the subject in her mind and is going to ask her something that is different from what her face says otherwise.

"With all this tension, how are you possibly going to persuade all of the other gangs to dissolve?" she asks.

"Because I'm going to figure out who did it," Tessa replies confidently, watching the people leave through the track gate.

"How?" Alonzo asks skeptically. Tessa puts on a pair of large, dark-rimmed glasses.

"What do you think?" she asks them. "Pretty gangster?"

Alonzo and Janet laugh. Tessa takes out a piece of paper with all of the chemicals she wrote down after she took a look at the bomb in the toilet stall.

"I'm going to match this chemical compound up with a problem set. It won't give me the exact answer as the one in the book but it will give me the same ingredients."

Alonzo and Janet exchange nervous looks.

"Do you want help?" asks Janet.

"Thanks," Tessa says, "But would you believe it if I'm not as stupid as my grades in class have made me out to be?"

"Fool, you could say that for anybody," Alonzo says.

"Yeah," Tessa agrees like it is the most obvious thing in the world. "You know, Yogun wants to be a basketball coach?"

"I didn't know that," says Janet. "How cool."

"I knew that," says Alonzo. "His secret dream."

"Hard to believe there could be something more important than his life that's at stake, huh?" Tessa says.

"What do you mean?"

"All year, we've seen what a person who doesn't live by the wake of their own dreams can turn into."

"Probably the kind of person we're saving him from," says Janet.

"Probably."

"You sure you can handle this?" Alonzo asks. "We can all study really hard and figure it out together."

Tessa nods to them before getting up. They can't help but be nervous because of how the life of their friend and mentor seems a little heavy to gamble on the depth of her wits.

"No, thanks," she insists. "This is something I have to do by myself."

Tessa perches the book down on the table in a private classroom, with all of the lights shut off and the fancy beakers and boilers set up. She turns on a single lamp shining like a lonely island of light. Closing her eyes for a moment before taking out a calculator, she begins attempting to recreate the experiment it took to make the explosive using a set of problems as a guide. A dusty moth flies on the page distractingly and then orbits its flight around the lamplight. As she continues to scribble down the formulas and boil up the chemicals, the fear of getting anything wrong quickly fades with an eerie recognition. This is something she has done before. She feels her hands close to the wounds of the underworld and can feel her own power to heal it. As she finishes uncovering the identity of the last chemical ingredient, the problem on the paper does not change. Her heart drums with a confusing thrill of excitement, the right answers are coming out but they brew a familiar compound from the past.

She scans her work again.

Every step she takes leads to the need of a similar formula she has seen before. Every element in this explosive is one from another homework problem – a very old homework problem. Suddenly this bright side of learning what she just figured out is rapidly eclipsed by the revelation that there is someone after her. Tessa closes the book. She then folds the notebook paper containing the chemical ingredients she found from the experiment and puts it into her pocket. For her own sanity, she momentarily elects to enjoy the relief of having the proof she needs, if only temporarily, to quell the tensions in the public sector. She rubs her eyebrow and squints into the dark.

No one is there.

Edin unlocked the door to the chemistry lab and found all of the cabinets opened. Someone had just done a haphazard job of cleaning it out and a good measure of Zionée's solvents had been used up. He went straight to Principal Flores's office. When he saw that the window was open, revealing the statue of Tessa outside, he was quiet. The breeze was chilly so Flores quickly closed it. She sat down, wrapping a collared jacket around her.

"Why did you have that built?"

"I thought it would be good for morale," Flores replied sarcastically. She gestured for him to sit down.

"You couldn't have said no to Abrams?"

"She's the superintendant, Edin. The people she doesn't like aren't usually in the most persuasive disposition."

"Are you afraid of her?"

"Edin," Flores started earnestly after a brief silence. "I did say no."

"Yeah. You would have."

She smiled back at him. Quickly, it faded, as his gaze guided her back to Tessa standing outside, despite her best efforts.

"How is she?"

"She's being strategically clever at avoiding me."

"I think I'm part of that," she said with a sigh. "Her strategy."

Edin was silent. The image of the dream Tessa's face began to flash in intervals of glittering sparks, merging with the one the statue now wore. There was something horribly wrong that he couldn't navigate his suspicions around. As though the evil had exited a human form and was now a much larger, incomprehensible force, as omnipotent as the darkening weather. He had an itch from the shirt label on the back of his jacket but he was too distracted to adjust it. It lingered like a faint tickle until he moved forward in his seat a little, pulling his chair closer to the principal's desk.

Flores read the crease in his forehead.

"Is there something wrong?"

Edin became really still before looking up at her. Suddenly, indignation arose within him, building from a year of unaccounted injustices against his only family.

"Why didn't you punish Rickward, Debby, Zera, and Cory for what they did at the beginning of the year?"

"I did."

"They should be expelled."

"It's up to me to decide what would teach them their lesson."

"Oh, yeah I'm sure they got it!"

He stood up from his seat.

"Young man, I'll have you written up for taking that tone with me!"

Her face was tough, her eyebrows flattened, and her red nose, shining from the cold, did not detract from the intensity of her gaze. Slowly they lifted with concern. She did not look away. It was the first time he had ever witnessed her exercise the full strength of her authority in that tough tone of voice. When he sat back down, she softened.

"Now tell me. Qué pasa?"

"I just feel like the wrong people are going to get way with doing bad things again," he said, frowning.

"Is there ever the right?"

They sat in silence, unable to read any further into each other except that there was a notion of things they could not reveal. Suddenly, Edin chuckled a little.

"Thanks."

"What for?"

"For feeling guilty."

"And how do you suppose that I am?"

"Just thanks," he said softly, appreciative of her.

Zionée walked up the stairs with Rigley on her way to period five. They arrived at the top floor of the private sector, both of them checking if the other was looking at the expression on their faces in the glass line above the lockers. Every time Rigley checked, Zionée would pretend to laugh and say hi to a friend. Every time Zionée checked, Rigley would be looking straight ahead or would be nodding to a classmate as well.

When she opened her locker to get their textbook that they shared turns bringing to class, he was surprised at how much emptier it had become.

"Hey, where'd all your Manga go?" Rigley asked.

The day before, she had received her privately assigned locker. Although they were so difficult to acquire at the beginning of the year where people had to share them, towards the end there were a few remaining because students gave them up from lack of use. After putting all of her Manga and Anime CDs in a new backpack, she put a lock around the zippers and then locked it all away with the combination folded up on a piece of paper. Her heart was racing at a maddening rate. She looked at his ruffled black hair and how a humor of light always glinted off the dark of his brown eyes. As he moved to stand up, he hit the edge of his own locker door, which he had forgotten to close.

"Are you all right?"

She couldn't help but break out and laugh. Zionée knew that the moment she would stop laughing now, was the moment it was going to be serious. He dropped his book on his foot after it missed the sleeve in his backpack and he quietly mouthed out in pain. Okay, maybe the next moment.

As they walked, her fingers kept moving closer and closer to his hand until it seemed less and less like a coincidence that she was brushing against it. He could feel the static between the hairs on their fingers sparking in intervals. At times, she put a little more distance, unable to bring her self to do it. But then she remembered the number of the error ratio on the note pad. For the past several days now, on the way to class, she had chosen to walk through the main hallways rather than go across the grounds where she would have to face her. In this intimate charade, the school seemed as though her home, her mother was the statue, and the hallways was her quiet escape avenue to her room to avoid being grounded.

Zionée stopped Rigley on their way to his locker, looking at him. She concentrated everything she hated about him into that look, everything about him that she detested. Then they continued moving without saying anything. When they got there, Rigley looked up at her once while taking his sketchbook out of his backpack and then stopped what he was doing.

"You're doing a lot of staring at me today without saying anything and it's really freaking me out. Not that it isn't nice to have someone stare at me when they're... well, when they look like you."

"Huh?" Zionée said, blushing but laughing this off. She became very still and quiet until Rigley sat down next to her. He shook his head. She sat down too.

"I've underestimated you," she suddenly said. "You're actually a lot smarter than me in some ways."

"Yeah?"

"Have you seen the statue outside?"

Rigley nodded slowly before turning away, looking troubled.

"I think they're trying to use Tessa to turn Edin against me."

"What makes you say that?"

She nodded, biting some dried skin off of her lip and chewing it.

"Because the destruction of our team wouldn't be complete without him."

Rigley looked at her.

"But through him. They can turn me against you."

She looked at him.

"But we won't fall for it... I mean, even just to pretend would be..."

"Egocentripetal motion?"

"More than I know how to handle. Like I said. I'm not as smart as you in some ways."

"It's not usually about being smart when it comes to that. But I suppose you're right."

She nodded. Her budget of words ran out again but her mouth was far from dry.

"That is how we'd have to play it."

His phone rang from an alarm tone he set and he took it out and started singing with the Japanese pop lyrics that his ringtone emitted. Zionée joined him and they both sang together in Japanese.

"All right, all right," they finished, singing the only verse in the song that was in English.

Before Rigley could stop laughing, Zionée rushed in and eclipsed his face with her own, capping her lips over his but shared the breath between them until they met. They both melted out of themselves. Rigley's eyes were wide with surprise but she kept her own closed, determined to lose herself to the feeling, and fully convicted to the knowledge that this is all the happiness of the moment she had left to enjoy between them before the predictable arc of romantic love would destroy the rest. The moment lasted in a small dewdrop of a cyclical eternity and when she finally pulled away, their faces were only an inch apart and she knocked her head against his with excitement. It was as though they had never been used to any other distance before. In exchange for what they now recognized in their hearts, they lost their recognition for their faces. They had become a completely different flavor of people to each other, turning to poison to all they were before but of the sweetest kind. Their lips pulled apart in slow, slow motion. Rigley could feel the bit of her dried lip skin in his mouth. Zionée blinked dry her eyes and held his hand as he stood up slowly. She stood up too, pressing her forehead against his. They were listening to the feeling of one another's breaths against their lips. Their eyebrows frowned upwardly. It was to begin. The venomous coursing of hormones soon began to take hold.

"What are you doing?" he said, pulling away.

"Because I absolutely despise you," she whispered with a smile and she kissed him again.

12 – AP Exam Season

It's my first day of school and I soon find out that it isn't as hard to make new friends as I thought. They wear clothing that is tattered and in sizes as exaggerated as their insults. The taunting seems playful at first. But then they start attacking past the clothing. Their humor reaches skin first, for all colors comes a stereotype negatively charged enough for a few laughs. And then, going past that, they start digging at what's inside, choice in sexuality, in friends, in clothes, and charisma. What is charisma around here? I look to the table at where most of the laughs are coming from. I stop joining in and start observing and listening. The teacher quiets a few disrupters but doesn't say anything about the taunts, which quickly lose their innocence as they start coming equipped with so much profanity. More than I've ever needed to use at my angriest but spoken very casually. The light is dim up above the ceiling. The tagging is like insects littered on so many surfaces that I can almost see it crawl. My heart is as light as I thought the humor would be at first. Five minutes in, I nod when I'm invited in on a joke about some kid and his silly hat. Ten minutes, I answer a question in class to make an effort of myself. I get it right and something changes in their eyes. Twenty minutes later, it feels heavier now, my heart. I can feel the hatred in their humor swirling like a dust devil towards where I'm sitting. Forty minutes later, they call at me only to set up a joke about my family. Fifty minutes past and I think the clock stops moving. I want to get out of here. As soon as I'm out in the courtyard, they throw something at the back of my head. The kids from my class apologize and it seems okay. But ten more days of this passes and the apology quickly goes out of fashion and memory. Ten days later, they take two heavy books I had to wait hours in line to get after several people cut in ahead of me. I'm shaking and I know what to say back but I don't say it. My mind can't think quicker than the hate in their eyes now burning in me. But my heart gets ahead of it and I hit and get hurt and the impact shakes me to the bone but suddenly I'm conscious of how stupid, how stupid I must look in front of them. They're all watching now. I drop my books and they kick it out of my reach as I stumble towards it. I'm not used to it, this hate. It makes me want to kill them. It makes me want to be them. My chemicals from my class assignment slip out of my backpack and fall on the books. The combustion ignites the leather-clad bindings. They stop laughing and start making mocking noises of shame. A small, thin string of azure falls before my face. The books burn brightly at first but the reaction is more dangerous with time. The dark, smoky clouds hover high above me. Come on, rain. Let it rain fast. The blood from the cut above my eye slides across the bridge of my nose. They run away as I'm left on the ground next to the grass surrounded by the flaming books. The flames turn blue. The clouds grumble with lightning and I feel a single, light droplet like a bubble sticker changing colors because of the blood on my hand. Finally.

AP exam weeks came. I had to go and purchase a few exams directly from my counselor and when I ran out of money, she lent me a couple dollars to make up for it. Thanks Mortinez, I owe you for that. On Tuesday, I had a study group meeting for the practice chemistry exam. Arriving forty minutes late, I could hardly keep up with anything they were talking about with the moles and the titration topics flying over my head. All this made me think about was the chemicals they used to make urethane, which is what I needed to replace on my skateboard. I went with my friend to change the wheels last Tuesday but had to quickly get back to studying before I could use them. After leaving chemistry, I had to make my way to period six for our last chapter test on Spanish. I could feel my mind biting hold of the new verb conjugations that I was memorizing last-minute by the time I got there, but it was still thinking about how many moles of iron was in 14 grams of iron sulfate. As I began taking the test I couldn't even hold my pencil straight in class. Edmondo muttered something in Letitia's ears and they snickered after looking in my direction. It seemed that everybody had already known.

Although it was nice and bright out, I could feel the cold, spring winds break through the threaded pores of my jacket. All I could see were the dark, red, apocalyptic skies rumbling with the threat of meteors. Even if the distance we decided to keep only strengthened the flavor of these poisoned kisses, I was ready to take full advantage of it. I stayed up as late as I liked, skating around parks and drawing anime, carving truth with urethane and lead until only a few shades of dark blue from sunrise remained. Then I would race the blood to my heart getting my homework done before the day began and it was due.

In history, Nairs threw me out of class twice in the past week, once for falling asleep and then for apparently cracking a joke in my sleep. Hashim later told me it was really funny. In science period, Weavins was frantically sending kids out left and right if they had just come up to ask him a question on the test. As usual, he would ignore me when I asked him how well this worked in past school years. In math period, we looked at all of the 11th and 12th graders exam reports on Professor Xen's desk. Most of them were crumpled and deformed origamis.

"Maybe he just folded them on too much caffeine?"

"Maybe you should shut up," Letitia said, scowling at me. Her scarf was tucked inside her vest and it looked like she didn't have time to apply makeup this morning. Right, fashion meltdown meant her sociability isn't the best.

In English period, Professor Tammy didn't care to make any latecomers slam a rhyme anymore to humiliate themselves in class. I ran in about five minutes late with a grime beat all ready. Instead, she handed me a pack of 11th grade practice AP exams from last year to deliver to the other English class. On my way down the hall, I took a peek at the grading rubric, which stressed a strong organization of concise thoughts and ideas.

Later at the library, I noticed Zera and Hashim at the library trying to hit as many books as they could for both their team GPA and their AP exams. After Hashim left to go purchase his AP exams, Zera walked with me on our way to art class to avoid Cory. Suddenly I laughed a little nervously loud, which she mistook for insensitivity.

"You asshole," she accused me. "Were you listening?"

"No, it's just, do you think you could ever be friends again with someone who broke your heart?"

She sniffed and wiped the last wet light from her eye.

"It's like being at the edge of an event horizon, Rigley."

Edin had been acting unusual lately. Whenever I saw him, he was hiding his face and reading dictionary books full of words I didn't even know about. Looks like someone's going to be prepared for the SAT.

"What's wrong?" he asked me as we were walking to the cafeteria area.

"You first."

"I'm fine, you go."

I ignored the nervous sweat on his forehead and continued.

"Your sister's been acting…"

Edin stopped and interrupted me.

"Do you know how many times she's spun in her chair to get herself to stop thinking about you the past six days?"

"She's doing that ritual again?"

"I'm not," Edin said, dignified.

"How many times?" I asked.

"Enough revolutions to fill up an hour."

Suddenly it was never mind that she's only been screaming at me at the top of her lungs every time she's seen me. Never mind that the only way to shut her up has been to snog her senseless. Never mind that everything good we had going has been warped into all this weirdness. I had just about enough of Zionée hurting us with her demands and disappointments but when she begins to hurt herself then that is where I draw the line.

"Where is she?" I demanded.

He showed me his text message from Zionée. I took the recorder we had been communicating through, put on my earphones, and pressed play. The anticipated anger of her voice exploded in my ears. I hope she was listening to me too on her way there.

Rigley arrived late with my physics notes I asked him to take down in class to help me get ready for the practice AP. After reading how useful they were, I used them to wipe my sweat from my hundred-meter sprint. I came in fourth.

"Thanks for the towels, Rigs," I said before briefly kissing the anger off his face. I couldn't even feel his lips move with any shape of a retort. According to the sexology book I've been reading, this awful, tingling sensation should go away the further we go together in this thing they call a romantic relationship. As soon as we exit the infatuation phase we'll not be able to stand another moment of one another. That's when I'll have the engine I need for time traveling. That's when I'll have his heart.

No, I must concentrate on physics. I'm the youngest student to take it at this time and year. I must pass the AP. After I left physics class, there was still chemistry to study for. When I got home, I swooped open the AP Chem book to start working on the practice problems for the exam. Another glance over my shoulder told me it was only half-past eight. Must make a dinner that can power me through the whole night. Maybe some leftover turkey with minted spinach and ranch. Better make sure not to leave the fan on around the sheets of stoichiometry spread about. As late into the night as I worked, I couldn't waste anymore time spinning around in my chair exorcizing Rigley from my hormones. For one thing, I was turning my guts into a roller coaster park for all of the food I was digesting. For another, it was counter productive. Not to mention the risk I was running for being mistaken for such a gross lack of concentration. I read the problem and started to dig for all of the numbers and variables in order to figure out what kind of equation it was. But now I have a craving to read my Manga. No, be disciplined. It is locked away for good now. I felt a thin, paper protrusion in my pocket and realized the combination slip was still there. I mustn't take it out. Let it get lost in the laundry. Remember, it's the only thing on paper I'm not letting myself memorize right now. I am stronger than Rigley. I am stronger. They must be running all of the dramatic parts right now that the filler episodes are over with. I find myself doodling again. I have to stop drawing his face. I stared at my chemistry textbook like a guest I forgot that I had invited over. After spinning in my chair for another hour, I got up and was so dizzy from the world still whirling around me, that I stumbled and fell over. A silhouette helped me up and the voice that came from it was Edin's. His face was still in a little bit of a blur and I got so scared of it reforming into Tessa or something that I punched it.

"Shit! I'm so sorry! Are you all right?" I asked. After I helped my brother plug up his bloody nose, I took out my score report from my math test and showed him. It was a perfectly folded crane.

"Look at my origami."

He looked away as though ashamed. No, don't be ashamed. If you're ashamed, we can't be related. My mind's eye popped wide open and I was starting to see the world through the other side of my brother's heart. So this is what it feels like to be my little brother – my little underling. But at least this gives us something to relate to again. Then he looked past me at something, clutching the blood soaked tissues to his nose.

"Have you tried doing the marathon problem experiment lately?"

I shook my head.

"That's good. No point wasting time on that when we've got our AP's to study for."

"Yeah, it's a stupid game," I scoffed.

"What's that smell?" he looked at me oddly.

"…Egocentripetal motion."

I left my room in a frantic haste. It's time I settled this with Tessa once and for all – mono-y-mono.

Zera had just finished drying her eyes on her way out of the bathroom. The soggy light poured through the hallway. The rain of light showers continued to spray against the windows. During AP History, she was given a recorder from Letitia.

"What's this?" she sniffed.

"From Zionée. Gave it to me to give to you to give to Rigley."

Her curiosity brewed as her finger rested its weight temptingly on the play button. Letitia turned around and read her mind.

"They're passing the recorders between the people they trust only. Oh, and don't ask me why they would trust you."

"But what about the Team Ranking?" she asked. Letitia ignored her and went back to her notes. Zera scoffed. "Maybe they've just hit a point where it's actually more difficult to trust themselves than it is to trust others."

"This isn't about the competition. It's about your favorite thing in the world, Zera. It's about history in the making and if you want to give it to your friends and brew up more trouble to make life more interesting, go ahead. All I'd care to do is judge you. But what I also wouldn't do is betray their trust."

"Are you implying I would?"

"I'm just saying that if you did, it would bring you that much closer to the people who have done so to you."

"Shut up, Letitia," she scowled. "I don't appreciate you stepping on my wounds like that to make my conscience work."

Before she could chuck the recorder back at her, Professor Nairs walked between their desks.

"Recording lectures? Good idea."

Zera nodded and then kept the recorder between her fingers. Having been unable to find Rigley anywhere between periods three and four, she gave it to Edmondo who had class with him next. His jokes were a little lighter on her today considering how well publicized her misery was from her recent breakup.

"We're all stressing out on exams and those two lovers expect us to play telephone and pass their voice notes around when they can just do it themselves?"

"There's a reason they're using a recorder! They don't want to speak to each other," Zera said. "And it's not telephone. Otherwise they wouldn't need our help."

He took the recorder.

"Why do they need yours?"

"Like it's any easier asking you for help. Because all the crap you've been putting me through all year for being the Rigley of our team has totally gone over my head."

"You are," Edmondo chuckled. "But that's not as much of an insult as it used to be."

Zera looked at him, surprised. He put the recorder in his pocket and nodded reassuringly.

At the soccer field, he ran into Hashim, who was practicing his pacing for cross-country. His blue jersey hung loosely to his tall, thin frame as he shot past the other runners. Edmondo tossed the recorder to him.

"An apology? You couldn't even work up the guts to say it to me in person?"

"It's not our drama, princess," Edmondo told him, annoyed.

"So you're not sorry?"

"I know I was hard on Zera," he said, wincing but not from sunlight. "And maybe I made fun of you more because of the attention you've been giving her. Because you know what kind of jealousy that is."

Hashim looked down at the recorder, slowly catching his breath before looking off.

"The kind of a best friend?"

He laughed and continued to jog as Edmondo watched with a slightly crestfallen expression.

Hashim later found Zionée wrapping sports tape around her ankles by the bleachers and gave her the recorder. She took out her earphones and walked back into the locker room. Her angry screams echoed across the hall, startling all of the other female track runners. When she came back out, Zera was with her, who now had the recorder again. Then she sprinted off, stomping as though she was trying to break the ground beneath her feet, as they both watched her go.

"You shouldn't run like that," Hashim said to Zera. "It hurts your legs and only makes it difficult to sustain yourself for cross-country."

Zera looked down at the recorder and smiled at him.

"Here we go again."

"Here Rigley," said the usually asleep Eslamida.

Rigley took the recorder and pushed play. As if the explosion in his eardrums wasn't enough, he had to endure its echo from the speaker herself after math class in the small space between the bungalows.

"Why were you six minutes late to the practice exam? Don't you know that we're supposed to spend roughly a minute on each problem? So guess how many I got wrong? Six! 52 out of 58! That's six minutes wasted on thinking about whether or not you remember your commitment to our team!"

She turned and stormed away but then wounded right back to him and they kissed with destructive passion. As they did, they could hear a couple of classmates passing by, talking about someone stealing chemicals from a lab to make a bomb. Their eyes opened as their mouths fought to keep hold of one another. She pushed his accusatory tongue back with her own. The harder she bit his tongue, the harder he would bite back. Their jaw muscles were beginning to become strained from the building competition between the two. Later in the main building, after they finished rinsing some blood out by opposite water fountains, they wiped their mouths and took separate flights to class.

Rigley went to open his locker but discovered it was jammed. When he tried to open Zionée's, she had changed the combination. Frustrated, he took out his recorder again.

"Just relax, Rigley. Remember how you do that best?" Vicky told him over the phone. "Oh – whoops... Nooo!"

Rigley flinched and pulled his cell phone away from his ear quickly. She had dropped her phone in the water again. He made a note not to call Vicky during her water tennis matches anymore. Upon opening his schedule in class, he found that there was still so much material to study for and do.

On the day of his first AP exam, he was running on far less sleep than Tammy told her students to get before the test. He tripped over Cory's backpack as he was making his way outside of class.

"Sorry, my bad." Rigley smiled as he picked himself up off of the ground, careful not to slip on any of the fully dotted scantrons that had been spilled all over the floor from the backpack. Professor Tammy didn't say anything for the time being.

"Rigley?"

"Good luck?"

"Oh, say what? Aw, hell no! Good luck happened when I was assigned your English teacher. Hard work began when you became my student. So I hope you can tell the difference when you're sitting there, bubbling in the right answers with your number two!"

Rigley nodded and dashed out of there. He could still hear Tammy's voice echo from the classroom.

"Anybody else got the audacity to ask me for good luck?"

The exam was held in the interior of the school gym with rows and rows of tables folded across the basketball courts. He took his seat near the end and noticed Zera and Hashim sitting across from him. Their sleepless eyes mirrored his own.

"Everyone," the proctor's voice possessed the ethereal gym, "If you would now please raise your dividers up."

They smiled encouragingly at one another and lifted their recycled science fair boards up. Rigley stared at the back of it for a moment, which had the picture of a kid next to his father. Then he lifted his board up. From behind their dividers, he could hear Hashim and Zera.

"I bet a lot of them already know about it."

"I think it's stupid that Flores isn't telling anyone."

Rigley closed his eyes and was a little guilty of thinking how if the bomb happened, then they wouldn't have to take the remainder of their exams. But it certainly wasn't worth endangering the lives of fellow students over. The light from high above the caged, gym windows cascading down on them started to darken.

"Yeah, my mom wants me to leave school early today."

"Think we should tell Rigley?"

"Of course, we should tell all of our friends about it."

Rigley was still as he blinked, unconscious of who he was for a moment.

"Everyone," the proctor announced. "You may now start the exam."

He ripped open the plastic bag that contained the booklet and turned to the instructed page. Next, he took out a sharpened number two pencil and began reading and bubbling in. As he worked carefully, he made sure that he was spending the correct amount of time on each problem. He worked through the shorter passages first; underlining sentences like a detective to match what each of the questions were referring to. Then he took his time with the essay question but saved just enough to go back. After doing a quick double-checking skim over the exam, he closed the book.

"In five minutes, please put your pencils down," said the proctor.

Rigley checked if he bubbled in all of the right college codes for the school he wanted to get credit for.

"Time's up! Please put your pencils down as we collect your college code booklets."

As one of the test administrators walked towards his desk, he frantically tried to bubble in the code for one last college he wanted to send his scores to.

"Hey, I said put your –"

An eraser flew up in the air from behind one of the science boards. Rigley looked up and laughed breathlessly, not sure whether it was Hashim or Zera. The test administrator turned around.

"Who threw that?"

One by one, in consecutive order, several more erasers were thrown up from behind the divider boards, buying Rigley the time he needed to correctly re-enter the code.

In the first floor hallway of the main building, Edin walked to class with a weight of dread slowing his pace, not especially concerned about being marked late in that evening of silver skies. He savored the solitude that being in motion afforded him. Suddenly Principal Flores walked up to him and whispered.

"So you've heard about the bomb threat?" she began.

Shuffling the mental pictures of Zionée's missing chemicals out of his mind with great difficulty, Edin nodded. The clicking of her heels made him start moving at her hurried pace.

"And?"

"So you must be thinking how stupid it is for me not to have announced it by now."

"It is pretty stupid," he agreed.

"I want to. Of course I care about the well being of my students. But on the off-chance that I'm wrong the school board is pressuring me not to act until I know for sure or else the shutdown can't happen until the last day of APs."

"There are a lot of off-chances of being wrong today, Principal Flores. But none of them will come out of the cost of anything worse than 1/4th points off an AP test."

"That is only if you choose to answer the question. And I can't afford to skip it."

Flores put her palm on to her forehead and for a moment Edin couldn't tell her apart from being another stressed out student.

"Hey!" he whispered as they started up the flight to the second floor.

"What?"

Edin stopped midway up the empty stairway to make sure that they were alone.

"I know for sure. That there's a threat of a bomb going off."

"How do you know that?" Flores asked, looking shocked.

"Because certain chemicals are missing. I can't tell you who they belong to."

Flores shook her head angrily.

"Why not?"

"You'll suspect it was them!"

"Do you?"

Edin stared back truthfully.

"No."

"Then why do you feel the need to protect them? Edin! You know I have to call you in for questioning for this. Oh my goshers! You are in so much trouble!"

He gave her a look. It was blank at first but then his features started to contort. He breathed fast as though on the edge of a panic attack. Of course her official position made her obligated to suspect them no matter what she would choose to believe on her own. He was suddenly wiping his eyes. She pulled him into a compassionate embrace and soothed him dry.

"It's gosh," Edin said while they hugged.

"I know, but I heard Rigley say it once and I thought that's what all the cool kids say."

She let go of him and they both laughed weakly.

Edin wiped the corner of his eyes dry. At that moment, a great big aching sore in Flores's heart grew for the generations of students Edin's situation stood for. They were being pushed into an adult world sooner than their innocence could realize its own loss. The knowledge they sometimes carried, years ahead of those in their age group, was like a burden maturing them into cold and lonely geniuses with brilliant but guilty secrets.

Zionée was coming from her second AP test when Rigley got her message from Edin. They had both been following the sonic trail of one another's last recorded messages ringing loudly in each other's ears and guiding them to the arena they were destined to share. Tessa's statue stood tall like an iron referee modulating them both from tearing each other apart. By the time they walked up close enough to lock eyes, his brown timber before her green emeralds, they pulled their earphones off and continued where each of their recordings had left off. It was like a climactic nightmare at the end of a brief and fleeting dream. Every kiss and touch was brewed for this confrontation. Their recorders have given them the proper long-distance relationship effect, compacted into the past four weeks of stress and now unleashed. Soon, the furious hurricane of their increasingly loud argument began wounding up an audience of eyes. Students gathered to look on and point from a distance. At the mound, Debby and Rickward, and their friends looked on amusingly. Cory started laughing and then choked after Zera elbowed him in the stomach. Rickward and Debby stared at this but didn't say anything. Edmondo and Hashim exchanged confused looks when all of the cutters in the AP brunch line jumped out of the way in front of them. They shrugged and walked forward the much-diminished line. Back at the courtyard, the teachers joined the small crowd building around the ruckus. Flores and Edin caught sight of the affair happening outside of one of the classroom windows and they both started rushing out to the grounds.

The louder they shouted, the more impervious they became to the growing number of onlookers gathering around them as well as the constant ticking at the back of their mind.

"And it was all your fault! Your fault, Rigley! I've never been less than anything but number one in my life until I met you!"

"What happened to not forgetting what it's like? About not being better?"

"That was when I let you manipulate me into believing it was okay to be a failure with all of your passions and your stupid Anime –"

"Excuse me for obstructing your ability to lie to yourself!"

"It wasn't lying – it was EXORCIZING! And you screwed it up! You screwed it up!"

"I have risked so much!"

"What, your passion – your artistic soul? FUCK YOUR SOUL!"

Everyone around them gasped. Rigley stopped for a moment before recollecting himself.

"Where would yours be? Without me?"

She blinked and glanced at everyone watching them for a moment. Everyone was silent and anticipating.

"We weren't supposed to let them win us from our selves!"

"It's not them who won! I did! I won myself back! This is who we were destined to be to each other! We just needed to break our hearts together to realize it!"

"What?"

"I wasn't playing it smart at all," she said. "I was playing the opposite! Because that's how you make me feel and there was nothing I could do about it but to fall right into it and take you down with me!"

Rigley became quiet. The crowd was silent. She pointed at the statue.

"Because the only way to win her heart…. is by breaking yours!"

The sound of Rigley's next words were interrupted with an abrupt explosion that sent them both flying backwards into the ground like limp dolls. The second before the first lick of fire protruded from the Tessa statue, Zionée stared deep into Rigley's eyes with a terrible anguish and pain. Now, unconscious, wounded, and bleeding next to the smoldering debris of the once whole statue; everything made sense in the one still sleepless part of their mind: the ticking. It had been counting down, and they, in the furious escalation of their screaming at one another, had each chosen more or less to ignore that common little piece of sense that was warning them something was wrong. As the rest of their consciousness slipped away, all sound and light withdrew in the vacuum.

The students in the vicinity scattered in a panicking frenzy and the teachers all ran to the two injured bodies. Weavins and the other staff did their best to manage the crowds as their panicking stampede threatened to pour into mayhem out in the streets. Principal Flores and Edin had been running towards them when they too were blown back off their feet. The explosion was small but had taken out the entire stone sculpture, hatching free at last the spirit that was trapped within. For a moment, that seemed too quick for the human eye to perceive, a blue jay flying by caught a glimpse of the fire echoing the shape of its shell, scorching upward and tall like a human figurine, wrapping itself around the space that was no more before extinguishing itself in a flash.

Edin didn't close his eyes once during the whole way to the hospital. Should he blink even for a second, it would allow a shadow of a lid to replay the awful moment in his mind. He could not stop shaking. His foster parents met him at the hospital. Principal Flores put on a mask of professional calm and went up to speak with them.

Edin was the first to go in to see his sister, decidedly alone. Zionée had a minor concussion, a broken hand, and a splintered collar bone, all of which the doctor told him she would heal in time for their next year of school. They turned to the bed next to Zionée and discovered it was Rigley's. Edin went over to it and stared at the silent face of his injured friend. He had a concussion and a broken forearm as well as a small burn on his shoulder. Edin buried his face in his hands, waiting for the uncontrollable sobs to come. But when he felt a hand on his shoulder, he looked up. It was Vicky.

"I didn't mean for this to happen," he told her.

She pulled him into a deep hug.

"I think that's the popular sentiment in this ward," she said. "I wasn't the team counselor I should have been. I ignored you when you were clearly jealous of your sister. I ignored Rigley when he needed help. I'm sorry. You three really got unlucky with me."

"Not that unlucky," Flores reassured.

She slipped through from the other side of the curtain and waited with the two of them for any sign of wake.

When Zionée opened her eyes, there was a glass of bubble tea on the table.

"I told them you only liked that Asian stuff," said Edin.

He, Vicky, and Flores were gathered around her. They all had a fading humor in their demeanors. Something graver than her injuries must have happened.

"What is it? Is Rigley okay? Where is he?"

"He's fine. He's resting in the bed next to you." Vicky began.

"Edin? You didn't stop speaking again, did you?"

He smiled at her and shook his head.

"Vicky? How are classes?"

"Oh, you know... been keeping busy. Part-time job. Water tennis."

"Water tennis," Zionée chuckled.

Finally she looked at Principal Flores. Her smile faded.

"I want to hear the bad news now."

"Zionée..." she began, "The school's superintendant has persuaded the district school board to a consensus. Those who were closest to the explosion at the time are the most likely suspects of being responsible for it. It was completely and totally unfair. I got suspended myself for... The point is, they decided to rule it under an attempted suicide bombing."

"It wasn't us," Zionée argued limply without feeling. She was beyond the numb of the hospital morphine. She wanted to scream but found no strength to.

"Here's the thing," Flores's voice cracked. "It doesn't have to have been the both of you."

A horrifying, greedy sensation suddenly surfaced within Zionée to allocate all of the blame on to Rigley. A pardon from expulsion needn't be wasted on a student less academically driven than her. But as a nurse passed by them and she saw the cast sticking out of the curtains, her heart was overwhelmed with feelings of everything they've been through. She suddenly realized how much dearer he was to her now and how much dearer everyone was. Upon confronting the intense fragility of their lives and the time they had together, everything became a lot closer. It was what kept the universe from expanding. But Rigley was dear to other people too. She could hear his parents speaking to his sleeping body. Although they were speaking in a mix of Asian dialect, their concerned, pacifying voices was too much for her. But before she could begin feeling sorry for herself again, she stopped and took three blinks between Flores, Vicky, and Edin. It wasn't constant. It wasn't usual. But in that moment, she sighed slowly with a grateful sense of relief. And she realized how she had almost destroyed her own ability to understand this feeling had it not been for Rigley. She knew then what she was able to do to return the favor.

She closed her eyes for several moments, listening to her lifeline signatures rhyme with Rigley's in their respective monitors. When she opened them again, the others in the ward could see that someone new was looking through them.

"Hey," she said to Edin. "Do you still have Tessa's yearbook?"

He nodded, surprised. Flores raised her eyebrows.

"What are you planning?"

"Zionée Dunnelin is going to be expelled. But I need you to help me enroll someone."

They met eyes and transferred the understanding they intimately shared.

"I'll do my best," said Flores. "But, are you sure you don't want to look at another school? There are plenty of private schools that your foster parents can afford to send you to –"

Zionée shook her head.

"No, listen. Flores, I mean, Tiffanie. I need you to do this for me. Besides," she looked in Rigley's direction, "If someone like Rigley can go through it and survive to be the way that he is, maybe I can too."

Edin looked from the other two and then back at his sister.

"No, you can't –"

"Would you excuse us?" she said, looking at her principal and her team counselor.

They both nodded and walked out, leaving Edin to sit alone beside her.

"It drove me crazy, you know," she began. "Beginning of the year. How scared I was for you."

"Huh?"

She touched the condensation on her tea.

"I know I've always come off... something cold. But when you started high school, and then those rumors started too. About why you didn't speak. That I was some kind of psychotic bitch who was only using you to show off another part of me."

"It's okay," he said.

"I'm sorry that you came to think that. And when you finally told me that you think that too... But I don't."

"Huh?"

"When you were little, I kicked a basketball at the cupboard. And a shaft of wood fell and hit your head. And then we had a fight about it. And then you threatened to never speak to me again. After you woke up the next day, you said you didn't remember the fight but I knew you did. I knew you did. Hey, in some ways, those rumors aren't totally off. I wish they were. But I hurt you. And I still don't know how to say sorry."

"You don't have to."

"No. Not because, I don't want to," she pressed on. Her voice grew watery. "But because... I don't know how it would be enough. And I knew... even after all this time... you were only pretending to forget the reason you stopped speaking so that we could survive together. No matter how mad you were; how much hate I made you hold... I was never grateful enough to see you as a person who helped me grow strong and gave me something to protect and to show how to do things and to hold on to the edge with... while everybody else had their mothers and fathers to help them up. I know it can't make it go away. Not this kind of pain. Of messing up so badly, for so many years, making you as perfect in my image as I could, only for you to think that was all I wanted you for."

Edin was speechless and slowly shook his head. They were silent for a moment. Finally, she sighed shakily again as the monitor beeped.

"Edin. I know that there are things we mean to tell each other but don't. And sometimes we end up regretting that. I know you would want to tell me I shouldn't do this. But this time, I want us both to be in on it. I trust you. So listen. No matter what happens or whatever name I go under, listen. We are siblings. Tessa or not."

She put her hand on his head until he finally nodded.

"I'll find out who did it. I swear I will."

The school year was nearing the end of its orbit for the sophomores. The remains of the statue littered the ashy soil with silver dust heated by the explosion. Some of the windows nearby had to be fixed because of the cracks caused by small bits of debris. Many goodbyes were said with the warmest of regards between the privates and publics but none would be said to Zionée or Rigley. Edin walked through the hallways alone with the aura of what had happened protecting him from unwanted social contact. But he continued to speak and carry out his attempts at being a normal high school student in spite of the heavy regimen that his sister had trained him to get used to bombarding his time from outside events. Finally, for one rare weekend, he was able to attend an end-of-the-year party held by his teachers in the cafeteria lounge. When he arrived, everyone greeted him on a first-name basis despite how most of the students who came were a year ahead of him.

Edin sat down by a prop table where he half-expected the principal to walk up to him again. Instead, Edmondo, Hashim, and Letitia sat down around him.

"Congratulations, Edin" Letitia said. "You're going to be a tenth grader now."

"Though looking like a seventh-grader."

"Shut up, Edmondo."

"I meant that as a compliment."

Edin stared at the cake on the prop table with unlit candles and a "Get Well Soon" shining in strawberry syrup font.

"This looks pretty real. For a drama department prop."

"It does," Edmondo agreed slyly. "Doesn't it?"

"Yup," Hashim added. "It sure does. I wouldn't try to steal it or anything so that you could give it to your sister and Rigley at the hospital."

Edin smiled and then looked at a finger print smear in the cream frosting like a signature of the one missing cook among them. He turned and saw Zera, sucking her finger, and hanging out with her snob friends. She smiled in his direction and winked.

At a cafeteria table with no umbrella, Tessa finished watching Yogun's graduation ceremony on her own private camcorder and stopped it there, freezing the small rain of confetti. Alonzo, Marco, and Janet exchanged relieved looks.

"You did it," said Marco. "I don't know how you did it, but you convinced them."

Marco and Janet got up and walked to join the others for lunch while Alonzo lingered, noticing Tessa's quiet look.

"What's wrong, man?"

"I only figured out who didn't. I still have to find out who did."

"Who do you think it could be?"

"Whoever they are – a dangerously intimate knowledge of me exists at their disposal. Someone who could turn this world I worked so hard to save against me."

"Yeah, well, I think this 'world' has better things to do. You maybe rep now but isn't it also thanks to you that it doesn't mean much anymore?"

Tessa took out the old bandana in her pocket.

"Oh yeah. Sorry if dismantling the gang meant losing all of your friends."

"Nah, I'm still cool with them," Alonzo said.

"And me?" Tessa asked.

"Like I said. I'm still cool with them," he said.

Tessa smiled, grateful for his approval. He started to go back to the others at the adjacent umbrella table.

"Hey, one more thing. You know an Asian guy with this English sounding accent?"

"Yeah, he's a private, right? Emilio and Marco have spoken to him too, he's pretty chill."

Alonzo checked his phone.

"Do you know him?"

"No," Tessa smirked. "Just through rumors."

As he walked back to the others, she secretly rewound it just a little further, when she made sure that nobody around was watching. The tape stopped at a point where Zionée, Rigley, and

Edin were getting up from the ground with their bicycles after crashing for the first time. She looked around at the miniature apocalypse she had made in the wake of the dissolution of all the public sector's gangs. The underworld was now under the shadow of brighter clouds and calmer days. From the birth of its end, a new beginning would spring. The graffiti mural was closed off and relieved to the supervision of the school janitors for maintenance. Students among the public started to discover friends and groups, not for the sake of surviving violence or verbal assault, but to get to know someone outside of their own pain or interests. And though Tessa still had a place beside those in Yogun's old gang, they too had moved on to many new friendships.

Progress was at last paved. However, there was still an incredibly cosmic distance between the publics and the privates. And she wasn't about to be satisfied until she brought the whole school together. Only then could she reunite with someone and fix what was broken. She took out the old yearbook that was supposed to belong in her name but instead it was a more recent edition from the previous year. Flores had switched the covers for her to remind her who she still was inside. She flipped the pages to where Edin's and Rigley's photos were and she circled them in red.

About the Author

"All our lives we've been taught to ride the waves of other people's expectations. Other people's dreams. After a while the crest builds and builds and you lose footing on your own. And then you lose track of how many times you have to pinch yourself to wake up from the one that isn't yours. I'm my own crest rider. I may ride the expectations of others. But I never forget my own. Because I know whatever I'm going to fall in love with doing in this life, I'm going to be greatest at it! That's how I'll know the dream is mine."

I wish to add to what my character said rather than change it because he might find this out on his own in his later high school years. I realize, because of my family and friends, that knowing what I want to do and to be good at it isn't nearly enough. Speaking only for myself for now, I'll know when a dream is mine when I remember most the people who have helped me get there and when I can see how much I can do for others. This is why I'm forgoing the usual "about the author" summary and acknowledgements list this time. I rather talk about what I've learned than what I've done because there is still so much to do. There are so many people whose wings I want to fly under but for every hero with a name to a million fans, there is only one of everyone already in our lives who support us when we're invisible. Without them, looking up to people and wanting to surpass the incredible things they do has no meaning.

Street Endie is a pseudonym. The author is an alien from the planet Earth.